Still can't get enough cowboys?

Popular Harlequin Blaze author
Debbi Rawlins keeps readers in the saddle
with her continuing miniseries

Made in Montana

Since the McAllisters opened a dude ranch
catering to single women,
the sleepy town of Blackfoot Falls
has gotten a lot more interesting....

Get your hands on a hot cowboy with

#701 *Barefoot Blue Jean Night*
(August 2012)

#713 *Own the Night*
(October 2012)

#725 *On a Snowy Christmas Night*
(December 2012)

#736 *You're Still the One*
(February 2013)

#744 *No One Needs to Know*
(April 2013)

#753 *From This Moment On*
(June 2013)

*And remember,
the sexiest cowboys are Made in Montana!*

Blaze®

Dear Reader,

It's been a wild year for the McAllister family of the Sundance Ranch. For generations McAllister men and women worked the land, raised prime beef and faced obstacles with grit and resilience. So when the economy took a nasty turn, giving up wasn't an option. Even if it meant opening their doors to paying customers.

When Rachel, the only daughter, came up with the dude ranch idea, her three brothers were less than thrilled. After all, they were rugged cowboys all the way down to the toes of their boots, and proud of it. But bringing in steady money meant no layoffs. Little did they know Rachel would post pictures of her hot brothers on the dude ranch website and attract more eager single women than she could accommodate. One by one, the mighty McAllister boys fell under love's spell, until only Trace was left....

This is his story. He's the youngest of the brothers and the one I thought would be the most difficult to write. Good thing the perfect woman for him showed up. Sure, Trace is one of those guys who could charm the pants off a gal without breaking a sweat, yet he's no match for street-smart city girl Nikki Flores.

I hope you are all enjoying summer. I kind of wish I was spending it in Montana.

Regards,

Debbi Rawlins

From This Moment On

—

Debbi Rawlins

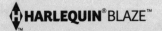

ISBN-13: 978-0-373-79757-8

FROM THIS MOMENT ON

® HARLEQUIN®
www.Harlequin.com

Printed in U.S.A.

ABOUT THE AUTHOR

Debbi Rawlins grew up in the country with no fast-food drive-throughs or nearby neighbors, so one might think as a kid she'd be dazzled by the bright lights of the city, the allure of the unfamiliar. Not so. She loved Westerns in movies and books, and her first crush was on a cowboy—okay, he was an actor in the role of a cowboy, but she was only eleven, so it counts. It was in Houston, Texas, where she first started writing for Harlequin, and now, more than fifty books later, she has her own ranch...of sorts. Instead of horses, she has four dogs, five cats, a trio of goats and free-range cattle keeping her on her toes on a few acres in gorgeous rural Utah. And of course, the deer and elk are always welcome.

Books by Debbi Rawlins

HARLEQUIN BLAZE
417—ALL OR NOTHING
455—ONCE AN OUTLAW††
467—ONCE A REBEL††
491—TEXAS HEAT
509—TEXAS BLAZE
528—LONE STAR LOVER††
603—SECOND TIME LUCKY‡
609—DELICIOUS DO-OVER‡
632—EXTRA INNINGS
701—BAREFOOT BLUE JEAN NIGHT§
713—OWN THE NIGHT§
725—ON A SNOWY CHRISTMAS NIGHT§
736—YOU'RE STILL THE ONE§
744—NO ONE NEEDS TO KNOW§

††Stolen from Time
 ‡Spring Break
 §Made in Montana

To get the inside scoop on Harlequin Blaze and its talented writers, be sure to check out blazeauthors.com.

This book is for my editor, Laura Barth,
who launched the Made in Montana series with me
and kept me on a steady course even when I wanted
to scream and hide. Thank you for your patience and
guidance. Good luck in your new position!

And for Brenda Chin...
thought you were rid of me, huh? Nice try.

1

"YOU HIT THAT YET?"

Trace McAllister didn't wait to watch the six ball sink into the corner pocket. He stepped back from the pool table, and with a bad feeling he knew who Sam meant, turned to follow his gaze.

Of course it was Nikki.

After delivering a pitcher of beer to the men waiting their turn to play, she was walking toward the bar. The close-fitting pink T-shirt tucked into her tight worn jeans showed off her small waist and curvy hips. She'd left her shiny dark hair loose tonight, falling halfway down her back. Hard for a man not to take a second, even a third look. Trace understood, but making a remark like that...

Nope. No way he'd let it slide.

The Watering Hole was crowded for a Thursday, though it was warm even for June, and every cowboy in the place had either a frosty mug of beer or a bottle in his hand. Two of the handful of Sundance guests, a pair of blondes whose names Trace couldn't recall, hovered near the end of the bar talking to a wrangler from the Double R. A tall brunette in a short skirt leaned over the jukebox, studying the selections.

So just to make sure he wasn't getting worked up for nothing, Trace asked, "You don't mean Nikki…"

"Hell, yeah. Look at her." Sam tipped back his beer bottle, draining it while his eyes stayed on Nikki's rear end. He wiped the back of his arm across his mouth. "That's what you call U.S.A. prime. Give it to me straight, McAllister. You do her yet, or what?"

"Are you serious?" Another remark and Trace wouldn't be able to hang on to his temper. He didn't know Sam all that well. He worked as a hired hand at the Circle K and had a reputation for being popular with the ladies, not so much their fathers. Trace had done his share of getting around, but he knew how to be respectful and discreet. "You know she's Matt Gunderson's sister."

"So?"

"So lay off." Instead of lining up his next shot, Trace looked Sam dead in the eye. "That's not a suggestion."

Sam leaned against the wall, chalking the tip of his pool cue, and giving Trace an amused look that aggravated him further. "Must be nice to have a rich family and the second biggest ranch around. Guess you figure that entitles you to speak down to the rest of us."

If he wasn't so pissed, Trace would've laughed. Man, Sam had it wrong. The Sundance had once been a nice spread, still was, with over three-thousand acres of choice land and a nice healthy herd. But they hadn't escaped fallout from the economic downturn. Most folks around Blackfoot Falls knew the McAllisters had converted part of the Sundance to a dude ranch in order to weather the storm. But then Sam wasn't the sharpest tool in the shed.

"Look, Sam, I've enjoyed shooting pool with you this week. And I don't wanna have to butt heads with you, but if you make another remark about Nikki, you and I are gonna have a big problem."

A short stocky kid who worked at the Lone Wolf moved closer to the far wall. Another guy left the back room. Trace had to motion for Lucas and Josh, two Sundance hands who looked as if they were itching to jump in, to stay out of it. Sadie owned the bar, and she had zero tolerance for fighting and foolish men in general.

"I knew you had it bad for her." Sam abruptly moved his hand. Trace tensed, ready to block a punch, but Sam only shoved his fingers through his long blond hair and grinned. "I wondered why you been coming to town to play when I heard you got a real nice table out at the Sundance."

Trace kept his face blank. Nikki had returned to Montana three weeks ago and had started at the bar a week later. He knew people were bound to put two and two together but most of the guys wouldn't say anything. Except for Sam, the pain in the ass.

"Admit it, McAllister, and I'll back off. Let you have her all to yourself."

That made Trace smile. The guy was dreaming if he thought he could get anywhere near her. Maybe he should let Sam find out what Nikki would do to a hound dog like him. The woman was small and beautiful, but she was tough. Get her mad enough and she had a mouth that could make a sailor blush. She also knew how to swing a two-by-four. Trace had seen it for himself.

"What the hell you grinning at?" Frowning, Sam glanced around, saw that the boys from the Sundance hadn't made a move. He seemed to relax and said, "You don't stake your claim, then I'm gonna have me a taste of that honey."

Trace really wanted to plant a fist in his face but he saw Nikki coming toward the back. No time to smooth things over, and he sure didn't want to start a fight, not in here. Sadie would probably ban him from the place. Knowing he was taking a risk, he waited until Nikki reached them, then he leaned his cue against the wall. What the hell…he could keep a straight face and the odds were in his favor.

"Go ahead, tell her what you just said." Trace folded his arms across his chest and smiled a little, just enough to make Sam second-guess himself.

He squinted at Trace, trying to gauge whether he was bluffing or really did know something Sam didn't. The fact was, since his sister and Nikki's brother had gotten cozy, Trace knew Nikki better than anyone in the bar, which wasn't saying much, but made for a hell of a bluff.

"What?" Nikki held her empty tray against her hip and looked expectantly at Sam. "You wanted something?"

He shot her a glance but didn't answer. The other hands were still hanging around, waiting to see Sam turn tail. They all knew him, and had probably arrived at the same conclusion as Trace. Sam couldn't afford to bring on Sadie's wrath. The Watering Hole was his hunting ground. He'd already gone through the eligible local women, been threatened with an angry father's shotgun—twice—so that left him with the Sundance guests. And this was the best place to meet the new batch of single women who checked in each week.

"I don't have all night, Sam," Nikki said, impatience flashing in her brown eyes.

They looked darker in the dim bar lighting. Normally, if he looked closely, Trace could see gold flecks. That is, when he wasn't fascinated by the shape of her wide generous mouth. He liked the way her lips turned up slightly at the corners.

"Another beer," Sam said, moving closer to her, and when her eyes narrowed in warning, he stopped and set his empty bottle on her tray. "Please, darlin'."

"I hope you're not driving." Her gaze slid over the front of his Western-cut shirt to the sloppy untucked hem. "Are you?"

"Ah, you worried about me?"

"No," she said with a short laugh. "I don't want you running into anyone."

Trace smiled. The other guys chuckled.

Sam had to be about six-one because Trace was only taller by an inch or so. And Nikki was on the petite side, maybe five-four. So when Sam leaned toward her, it was hard to guess his intention, but he was asking for trouble no matter what he had in mind.

She tensed, and so did Trace.

Sam whispered something in her ear, then slowly drew back, a stupid grin on his face.

Nikki shook her head. "You keep on dreaming," she said in a dry tone. "See how that works out for you." She turned to Josh and Lucas. "Y'all want another beer?"

Her slight Southern drawl came out when she was irritated or excited or caught off guard. Trace didn't have to guess at how she was feeling right now. She didn't care for Sam, which seemed hard for the idiot to believe so he'd continued to make a jackass out of himself.

Trace watched her finish taking drink orders, collect empties and then start to leave. "What about me?"

She arched her brows at him. "What about you?"

"I need another beer."

"You still have half a bottle left."

"It's warm."

Eyeing him with suspicion, she made room on her tray as he walked over to give her the bottle. "You do this all the time."

"Do what?" He reached for his Stetson before he remembered it wasn't sitting on his head but on a wall peg in the corner. To cover the gaffe, he plowed his fingers through his hair. It was too long, hugging the back of his neck and curling at his collar.

"Tell you what," Nikki said, her gaze fixed on his hand

before slowly moving to his face. "Switch to tap. I'll give you half a mug at a time and ask Sadie to charge you for a kiddie portion."

Sam laughed, and so did the rest of the guys. But Trace didn't care. Nikki hadn't looked at any of them the way she'd just looked at him. The heat had lasted only a moment. If he'd blinked he would've missed the flicker of awareness in her eyes, the brief parting of her lips as she tipped her head back to meet his gaze.

"I'll stick to bottles, and don't worry about me leaving some behind." He leaned in just like Sam had and whispered so only she could hear, "I do have to drive."

She reared back and looked at him as if he'd lost his mind, then let out a startled laugh. "Maybe I should cut you off now."

Better she thought he was being weird or tipsy than figure out he was trying to outdo Sam. Everyone was quiet, stepping aside to clear a path for her, though any minute Josh and the other hands were gonna bust from curiosity. Same with Sam, even if he was trying to appear cool.

Fighting a smile and shaking her head, Nikki left to fill their orders. He wished she'd laid one of her rare but dazzling smiles on him. He could've gotten a lot of mileage out of that, but Trace figured her answer was vague enough that he'd be able to mess with Sam a while longer.

Already Trace was paying for his mischief. She was halfway across the bar yet he could still smell her. Just like her sexy almond-shaped eyes and lightly golden skin, her scent was exotic, kind of mysterious. It seemed to cling to his shirt, the walls, the air around him. No wonder his pool game had been crap lately. His concentration was shot. Sure didn't help that he couldn't seem to drag his gaze away from the sway of her hips.

He'd finally convinced himself to return to the game when he saw a Sundance guest call Nikki over to her table. The woman's name was Karina, which he hadn't known until tonight, and only because she'd been hanging around the pool room earlier. She'd arrived yesterday and was blonde like so many of the guests, but easy to distinguish since she towered over all of them.

She wasn't just tall, but close to six feet kind of tall. Behind her back Sam called her The Amazon, but mainly, Trace suspected, because he'd made a play for her and she hadn't been interested. Trace liked her fine. It was refreshing to have a guest who actually wanted to watch a game of pool and not breathe down a guy's neck.

Nobody in the family had wanted to go the dude ranch route. Both his brothers had hated the idea. They were all cattlemen, just like every McAllister man before them. Swallowing their pride left a bitter taste, though Cole and Jesse got off easier than him.

Cole ran the cattle operation. He'd barely turned twenty-one when the reins were passed to him the day after their father's funeral. Jesse had been in college at the time, and Trace and Rachel still in high school. The sorry state of the Sundance had nothing to do with Cole's management and everything to do with the economy. In the end, Rachel had been right to push the dude ranch idea to bring in cash. But that didn't mean Trace liked being her flunky when it came to entertaining the guests. All of them female, because that's who Rachel targeted.

When they'd first opened and the women had come pouring in, Trace had a blast. Women of every shape and size literally landing on his doorstep? It was heaven on earth. Now, ten months later, he was jumping at his own shadow and hiding in the stables like a skittish colt.

Karina said something to Nikki, who nodded and glanced over her shoulder. At him.

He could've kicked himself into next week for getting

caught staring. Leo, who owned the filling station at the south end of town, was sitting at a table behind the women, and Trace lifted a hand to him. The older guy frowned, then grudgingly lifted a hand in return, probably wondering if Trace was drunk.

"You gonna play or what?" Sam sounded irritable. "Plenty other guys are waiting to take your place."

"Yeah, I mean, no, go ahead." He nodded at the cue he'd left leaning against the wall. His mind wouldn't be on the game. No sense going through the motions and holding up the others.

"We're not finished," Sam said. "Afraid I'm gonna whip your ass?"

"That's right." Trace snorted. "I bet you still believe in Santa Claus, too."

Sam cursed under his breath. His mood had gone south fast and no one would want to play him. "Who's up?" he asked, looking around the room.

"I'm just watching," Josh said, and Lucas shook his head.

The guy from the Lone Wolf didn't say a word, just sipped his beer. Trace didn't know his name but nodded to him, and he gave him a friendly nod back. Matt Gunderson had returned to run the ranch since his father had been confined to bed, and Trace wondered if Matt had sent the man to keep an eye on his sister. Probably not. Nikki would catch on and be mad. Then again, it wasn't likely she'd recognize one of the hands.

Although she'd been living at the Lone Wolf since her return, according to Matt she wanted nothing to do with the place. Or their father, for which no one in town would fault her. Wallace Gunderson was a despicable human being. But as his illegitimate daughter she was a Gunderson by blood, if not in name, and entitled to half the large ranching operation upon Wallace's death. Which apparently was fast approaching.

Trace chanced a look and saw that she'd slipped behind the bar to fill mugs of beer while Sadie was busy pouring shots. Almost as if she sensed he was watching, Nikki swung a look at him. Neither of them broke eye contact right away, but then she had to stop the mugs from overflowing.

She did a good job of acting indifferent toward him, but it was mostly pretense. He might've thought it was his ego overriding his brain but his sister had confirmed Nikki had a soft spot for him. Though Rachel hadn't meant to give him hope. In truth, she'd been warning him that if he played fast and loose with her boyfriend's sister, she'd wring his neck.

He supposed she had some cause for concern. He'd always been lucky with women, and a number of them considered him a big flirt, but usually because they flirted back or initiated the dance. And Rachel sure hadn't been shy about exploiting his so-called easy charm to help her keep the guests happy.

But with Nikki he'd been careful from the moment he'd met her in February. At first because she was Matt's sister, and then because Trace had seen the cracks in her cool facade. They'd sat right here in the Watering Hole after a drunken idiot had accosted her outside. Matt had arrived in time to stop the guy, but the idiot's friend had joined the party and Matt ended up with bruised ribs, a swollen face and lucky to still have teeth.

Nikki had been quick to accept the blame for her brother's beatdown. So quick, it had stunned Trace. She'd been a victim as much as Matt, but all she'd been able to see was that she'd brought him trouble and that was all she'd ever do. She hadn't come out and said it like that, but in those few unguarded moments, Trace had listened well. And he'd learned three things about her that night: she was fiercely loyal to people she cared about, didn't trust easily and liked to keep her emotions tightly wrapped.

He knew she'd had a rough life growing up in Houston. Being raised by a single mother who'd worked two jobs to support them wasn't a tragedy in itself, but Nikki had hinted that as a teenager she'd gotten into some trouble in her gang-infested neighborhood. She hadn't elaborated, and it was pretty clear she'd regretted being so open.

Other than that night when he'd looked after her while Matt got patched up, Trace hadn't spent any time alone with her. She'd come to Blackfoot Falls because her brother had wanted her to meet Wallace and get closure before he died. Matt also hoped she would like Montana and move to the Lone Wolf. They'd stayed two weeks and then Matt had to return to the rodeo circuit and Nikki to her waitressing job in Houston.

And in those three months they were gone, Trace had thought about her every single day. He'd never been that dogged over a woman before. His last new truck, yeah, and technically it hadn't been new. But he'd thought about that honey every day for over five months before he had enough cash to bring the Ram home with him.

"Hey."

Trace snapped out of his preoccupation the same time Nikki touched him. He looked at her small hand resting on his forearm, at the neatly trimmed nails that had a light sheen but no color. Then he looked into her pretty brown eyes that had seen too much. They got to him every time.

"You were daydreaming." She drew back her hand. "If you had knocked this tray over I would've strangled you. Here."

He took the bottle from her. "Thanks."

"Don't thank me." She motioned with her chin. "Thank your friend sitting near the jukebox. The beer's from her."

His stomach turned. "Karina?"

"Yep."

"I don't want anyone buying my beer. Tell her I said thanks anyway."

"Tell her yourself." A small smile tugging at her lips, Nikki turned to pass a mug to Josh.

"I'm serious. Add this to my tab and then I'm cashing out."

"You're leaving?" Disappointment flickered in her eyes, and then she blinked and it was gone. "I can give you a total now," she said, all business. "You've had, what…two beers?"

"This one makes three." He waited for her to meet his gaze but she was being stubborn. He really didn't want to leave yet, and if she gave him the slightest indication she'd like him to stay, he'd wait for her to get off work. But no, she seemed determined to treat him like he was any other customer. Which he supposed he was, but sure didn't like it.

He set the bottle down and dug in his pocket. For over a week he'd had the same thing every night so he knew his tab came to $9.75. He pulled out two bills and laid them on her tray. "Keep the change."

"Isn't Karina a guest at the Sundance? You really want to turn her down?"

"Yeah, I do." He wasn't about to let that bronc out of the chute. Bad enough he had to socialize with the women crawling all over the Sundance. He didn't need to owe any of them.

"It's just a drink, Trace."

He smiled. No, it wasn't, not with these women. "Your next day off, how about you and me take a drive to Kalispell?"

"Why?" She glanced around, but no one had heard. He'd made sure he kept his voice low, and Sam was busy racking balls for the next game. "Isn't that forty-five minutes away?"

"You haven't been, right? It's nice. Lots of restaurants, bars, department stores, movie theaters. I think there might even be a bowling alley."

"So…you're asking me to go because…?"

"I don't know." Man, she didn't make it easy. "I have

business there, anyway," he said, lying through his teeth. "I thought you'd like to check out what's available…stuff we don't have in Blackfoot Falls."

"I appreciate the thought." She picked up two empty mugs off the shelf that ran along the wall. "But I have a bunch of things to do when I have time off." Now she was lying. She wasn't any better at it than him.

"Okay." He saw Sam eyeing them, curiosity coming off him like steam. "If you change your mind let me know." Trace grabbed his Stetson off the peg and returned his nearly full beer to her tray. "And don't worry, Nikki. It's just a drive."

2

NIKKI FLORES WATCHED one of the blondes who'd been sitting at the end of the old mahogany bar run for the door that had barely closed behind Trace. Another woman had stopped him before he'd even made it that far. Whatever she'd said had him shaking his head, but he'd flashed her that movie star smile of his, the kind that had silly women forgiving and forgetting when they should be slamming doors shut.

"You gonna sulk the rest of the night because he went home early?" Sadie set a pitcher of beer on Nikki's tray.

"Me?" She rolled her eyes. "No, but his fan club might. If we're lucky they'll drown their disappointment in expensive cocktails. I say we raise the price of those stupid appletinis."

Sadie chuckled, sounding much better without the rusty wheeze she'd had a few months earlier when Nikki had first met the older woman. A lot of Nikki's traumatic first visit to Blackfoot Falls had blurred once she'd returned to Houston. She'd only remembered a few things…the beauty of Montana wasn't something easily forgotten, and the air, so clean and clear that taking a deep breath actually made her head light.

And the McAllisters…Nikki had never met a family like them. Their warmth and kindness was part of the reason she'd agreed to come back with Matt. At first she'd been wary. How could all three brothers and a sister be that well-adjusted? But then she'd met their mother. An hour spent with Barbara was all it had taken for Nikki to understand them. Oh, they weren't perfect, not even close, but it was their unconditional love for one another and how they had each other's back that impressed her.

Sadie had also made the short list. Nikki had only talked with her a couple times, but the woman sure seemed to know when to speak up and when to keep her opinion to herself. Nikki had been a wreck the night Matt had gotten into a fight protecting her. Every instinct had screamed for her to find the guys and get even, show them they couldn't mess around with her or her family. Growing up, she'd learned to protect her own because no one else would.

But Matt had brought her to Montana so she could have a new life. Leave her troubled past behind. Sadie hadn't known her circumstances, yet she'd seen the thirst for payback in Nikki's eyes and in a few well-chosen words, convinced her it wasn't worth it. When Nikki thought about it now, she had to hold back a shudder. The people here didn't understand what she was capable of. Not even Matt got it. He hadn't known her as a teenager.

That same night Trace had come into the bar with her, and to be fair, he'd played a big part in calming her down. He'd sat and listened and told her he wouldn't blame her one bit for wanting to slap those guys into the next zip code. And then he'd reminded her that it wasn't over—the men would be fired and the pleasure should be Matt's.

God, it still bothered her that she'd told Trace little things about her past she wished she'd kept to herself. She'd known him less than a week, had never spoken to him one-on-one before that night. At the last minute he'd shown up to help Matt and ended up with a split lip. Not a big cut, just a small nick near the corner of his mouth. It had stopped bleeding pretty quickly, but every time she looked at him, she was reminded he'd been hurt because of her.

That was the only reason she'd opened up to him. Why she'd confessed that she hated Wallace more than she thought humanly possible, that he deserved to be sick, and how she was glad he was dying. She hadn't censored her vile thoughts. They'd tumbled out of her mouth, and Trace had just sat there, without a hint of judgment.

Of course some of it wasn't news to him. The McAllisters knew quite a lot from Matt because he trusted them. The scary part was, for those two rocky hours she'd sat with Trace, she'd actually trusted him, too.

That was enough to rattle her. She just didn't put that kind of faith in people. She trusted Matt, but getting there had taken nearly a year of ups and downs. The only other person she completely believed in was her mother, who loved her no matter what. Her mom was the main reason Nikki was giving Blackfoot Falls a try. She'd met a businessman from Mexico City who wanted to marry her. But it wouldn't happen, she'd never leave Houston as long as Nikki was there.

No, trust didn't come easy for Nikki. Especially with men. They always disappointed her. And a guy like Trace with his looks, his family's clout, money and a bright future... He was the worst kind of man to count on. Good-looking smooth guys like him couldn't seem to help themselves. They had charm to spare and felt they owed it to the female population to spread it around.

She'd fallen for a man like that before, and she'd been burned. Badly. Just like her mom had been crushed by Wallace all those years ago. If nothing else, Nikki had learned a lesson from the experience. Or so she'd thought until that night she'd blabbed to Trace.

"You need anything else besides those tequila shots?" Sadie asked, with a glance at Nikki's loaded tray.

"No, this is it. Thanks."

"I wouldn't worry about Trace."

Nikki hefted the tray at the same time Sadie spoke and almost let the pitcher slide off. "Where did that come from?"

"You've been staring at the door the last five minutes. I figured you were worried about him."

"Why would I be? That's crazy."

Sadie smiled. "My mistake."

Nikki dropped off the pitcher first. She'd been carrying heavy trays and serving drinks since she was old enough to work. But something in Sadie's smug expression had thrown her off and all she needed was for the entire order to crash to the wooden floor.

Her tips weren't so good that she could afford to hand half over to Sadie.

She delivered the tequila shots to the two cowboys sitting in the corner and managed to give them a smile. They were nice laid-back guys whose names she really should remember. Both were good tippers and patient when she got slammed. She hated that all the other customers seemed to fade when Trace was in the bar. But what she hated even more was that he hung out with Sam.

Sometimes Sam was okay. He'd come in nearly every night since she'd started working for Sadie. He liked to flirt and tease, not just with her but with the Sundance guests. She knew that at least one of the women had gone off with him last week. For her part, Sam was the kind of guy she'd go a mile out of her way to avoid. He was good-looking, but too cocky and full of himself. Definitely a one-night stand guy. After checking on her customers, she stowed her tray and slipped behind the bar to wash glasses. The dishwasher had conked out three years ago and Sadie had gone without since. Last week she'd admitted to Nikki that she'd almost closed the bar a month before the Sundance opened their doors to guests. Business had gotten slow with so many layoffs in the area. The hired hands who were left had started going to Kalispell for their entertainment. Until all the young single women began arriving each week.

At the end of the bar Sadie made jukebox change for a customer and then grabbed a clean towel and joined Nikki. "I was gonna get to those glasses next, but thanks for pitching in. You're a good worker, Nikki. And God bless you, you showed up at the right time. I would've been up a creek without anyone reliable to fill in for Gretchen."

"She's ready to have her baby anytime now, right?"

"Next Tuesday is her due date." Sadie picked up a mug and dried it. "Claims she'll come back to work in two months but I've got my doubts. Even if she does I can still use you two nights a week if you're willing."

Nikki nodded, though she'd been hoping for something more full-time. But then again anything could happen in two months. Her mother planned on relocating to Mexico City in three weeks. As soon as she was settled Nikki could start thinking about where she wanted to end up.

Cole's girlfriend, Jamie, loved San Francisco, claimed it was one of her favorite cities, and she was a travel blogger who'd been around the world more than once. Maybe Nikki would go have a look for herself, see if she could find a decent job there. Although she was hoping to save more money before she left.

If she left. She really was trying to keep an open mind, but she couldn't seem to imagine the Lone Wolf ever feeling like home. The huge two-story house was beautiful, nicer than any place she'd ever lived or most likely ever would. And the guest bedroom, which was now hers according to Matt, was almost as big as the apartment she'd had in Houston.

Most of the time the ranch was quiet, too. So still and quiet that at first it had creeped her out. In her old neighborhood it wasn't unusual to hear gunshots in the middle of the night. Sometimes at the Lone Wolf if she kept a window open she'd hear a calf bawling or a rooster crowing. She hadn't gotten used to that yet.

"Do you think Marge might need help at the diner?" she asked, and Sadie frowned. "I'd still work here whenever you needed me, but after Gretchen comes back, I wouldn't mind picking up a few shifts over there."

"I don't think she needs anyone but it wouldn't hurt to ask. Frankly, though, I think the tips are better here." Sadie dried two more mugs before she said, "Of course I'd never refuse to take Gretchen back, but it wouldn't surprise me none if she wanted to stay home with that new baby and only work a couple nights a week. If that happens, the other shifts are all yours."

"Thanks. I appreciate it." She watched Sadie brace a hand on the back counter while she stretched up to stow the clean mugs on the upper shelf.

Her diabetes was under control, and she'd lost some weight, which allowed her to get around more, but she still had a few health issues. She'd been divorced a while and her only daughter lived in Oregon. For whatever reason, they rarely spoke and hadn't seen each other in years. Sadie only had the Watering Hole. Leaving her would be hard. Nikki hadn't expected that, especially not after working for her only two weeks. She'd miss the small rustic bar, too, with its warped tables and mismatched chairs.

"You look a little sad tonight, honey." Sadie took the soapy mug from her and rinsed it. "You missing your mama?"

"A little. Mostly I'm happy she's found someone who really cares about her." Nikki couldn't say the words without thinking about Wallace and how horribly he'd wronged her mother. She'd been young, hopeful and in love with the handsome older man who'd used her until she and Nikki had become an inconvenience.

"She have any family in Mexico City?"

"Some cousins and an uncle. I've never met them, but she's stayed in contact."

"I imagine you'll be visiting her soon enough."

Nikki nodded, though she worried she couldn't scrape together the money to make the trip. No way she'd accept the fare from Matt even though he'd offered. She still planned on repaying him for the money he'd secretly sent her mother for a year. He just didn't know it. Good thing, because it was going to take her forever.

"I hope I'm not opening a can of worms here," Sadie said, "but how's Wallace doing?"

Nikki shrugged. "He has a few weeks. He's not even seeing the doctor anymore. A nurse from the clinic stops by now and then. Matt and Lucy are taking care of him."

"Well, I sure give Matt credit. I doubt that boy ever heard a kind word from Wallace."

"I think in Matt's mind he's doing this for his mom."

Not anxious to talk anymore about Wallace, Nikki finished washing the last glass and then rinsed and dried her hands. "I'd better go check to see if anyone's thirsty," she said, her gaze going to the door. It had been a while since Trace left and the woman who'd chased after him hadn't returned. Nikki had no business wondering what they were doing. They could be making out in his truck for all she cared.

"I bet she asked him for a ride back to the Sundance just to get him alone." Sadie moved closer and lowered her voice. "Some of these city gals are downright shameless."

Nikki didn't bother denying her thoughts had drifted to Trace. Sadie saw too damn much. "Yes, sometimes we are."

"I didn't mean you."

"Sure you didn't."

Sadie gave her a long look and laughed. "Don't you start getting sassy with me."

"Well, I am a city girl. Before coming here, I'd only left Houston once." For a quick trip over the border to Mexico when she was sixteen and what a disaster that had been. Too late she wished the memory had stayed buried along with the other stupid rebellious things she'd done.

"Yes, but you aren't like them." Sadie's gaze flickered toward the tall brunette talking to Sam. "That one, Sam Miller, he's like a hound in heat. I'm not complaining, mind you. He's good for business."

"So is Trace."

Sadie didn't appreciate the remark, judging by her narrowed eyes. It was clear she liked Trace, maybe simply because he was a McAllister, no telling. "Those two names don't belong in the same sentence."

Nikki had to put her opinion on hold when a customer signaled for her. She'd meant to check to see who needed refills, not start thinking about Trace. Or trying to figure out how she could get information about him from Sadie without being obvious. Really stupid because she'd had him figured out the first night she met him at the Sundance. He'd been surrounded by fawning guests, eating up the attention. She'd promised herself right then she'd stay away from him. If she decided to hang around Blackfoot Falls for a while, she didn't want to be the subject of gossip and embarrass Matt.

While collecting drink orders she had the feeling of being watched and looked over to find Sam staring. He gave her a sly wink that made her want to smack him. She pretended she hadn't seen it. After working in bars for five years, she'd found it was best to ignore men like him when they were on the hunt.

"Four more tequila shots and three beers," she told Sadie, then slid her tray onto the bar.

"I think Sam was trying to get your attention."

"Sam can kiss my—" Nikki pressed her lips together.

Sadie chuckled. "I hate to tell you, honey, but I think that's exactly what Sam wants to do."

"Sorry," Nikki muttered. "He's a customer. I'll play nice."

"Not if he gets out of line, you won't. I'll take a switch to him myself. Though I reckon Trace would beat me to it."

She sighed at the woman's teasing smile. "Why would Trace care? They're friends."

Grunting, Sadie grabbed the bottle of tequila. "That'll be the day. That pool table is about the only thing those two fellas have in common."

"And being good for business."

"That, too." Sadie moved the shots she'd poured onto Nikki's tray. "Although I think poor Trace has been coming to town to get away from those city gals." Sadie didn't even try to hide her amusement. "More likely, though, he has his eye on a certain pretty new waitress."

"You're delusional and a troublemaker." Shaking her head, Nikki grabbed a stack of cocktail napkins. "Why does anyone want to work for you?" She ignored Sadie's laughter and picked up the tray. "Don't forget to check your blood sugar."

Sadie glanced at the round clock on the wall behind her. "Thanks, honey."

Nikki heard the soft gratitude in the older woman's voice and hurried off to deliver the drinks. Letting herself care too much about Sadie would be a foolish move. So would letting Sadie think she could depend on her. Right now she was so lost and confused she was no good to anyone.

NIKKI WAS FINALLY getting the hang of driving a pickup and she wasn't even grinding the gears so much anymore. No sooner had the thought formed than she shifted to make the turn onto the gravel drive and cringed at the awful sound she made. The truck Matt had given her to use was old and smaller than the other two big four-door, extended cab models that belonged to the Lone Wolf. He'd tried to convince her to take Wallace's Escalade, which was an automatic, but driving the luxury SUV scared the crap out of her. Even though she'd gotten her license at eighteen, she'd never owned her own car. In Houston she'd used buses to get to work, then always managed to find a ride home.

The Watering Hole didn't stay open late. Most of the customers were either hired hands or ranchers who woke up at an ungodly hour to take care of their animals. By eleven the bar was usually pretty dead. A few of the men stuck around if they had the next day off or were close to hooking up with a Sundance guest. No matter who was there, Sadie shooed them out and locked the door by midnight.

Something else for Nikki to get used to. Since she was eighteen she'd worked until the wee hours of the morning. Even while she'd attended community college for two years she'd worked late, and then studied when she got home. This going to sleep early crap wasn't easy.

Driving slowly toward the Lone Wolf she saw that the bunkhouse was completely dark. Only the low-watt security lights were on in the barns and stable. The house was a different story. Lights blazed from the foyer and Wallace's office, even the kitchen was lit up.

She saw Rachel's small white car parked next to Matt's black truck on the side of the house. No other strange cars were there, like one that could belong to the doctor, so she figured Wallace hadn't died. It still seemed weird living in his house. She never saw him…only twice in the three weeks since she'd come back with Matt. God only knew what Lucy, the housekeeper, or Rachel thought of Nikki for refusing to help with his care. She knew Matt understood why she'd have nothing to do with the bastard, and that was good enough for her.

The promise her mother had forced her to make still irritated Nikki. Why the hell did her mom care when Wallace finally passed on? He'd caused her nothing but misery. For two years before Nikki was born and three years after, he'd gone to Houston pretending it was business while he cheated on his wife. The arrangement might've lasted forever if her mom hadn't given him an ultimatum—divorce Matt's mother and acknowledge Nikki as his daughter. That was the last time they'd seen him.

Of course Nikki didn't remember him very well because she'd been too young. But it wasn't easy to forget the violent crying jags and gloomy weeks her mom had been too depressed to go to work. Nikki loved her with all her heart, but she would never be that weak. She'd die before she gave a man that much power over her.

3

NIKKI BURIED HER FACE deeper into the pillow. The windows were closed and she'd shut the blinds tight before she'd crawled into bed at four this morning. So where was the light coming from? And the noise… Outside men were talking while horses were doing whatever annoying things horses did…besides terrify her. How was a person supposed to get any sleep?

She blindly felt around the other side of the queen bed, found the extra pillow and plopped it on her head. It helped to mute the sounds but not enough. Oh, man, maybe she hadn't closed the windows. Her bedroom was too chilly. Even in June, at this altitude, the nights and early mornings had a nip in the air that had her thinking twice about staying for the week much less indefinitely.

With a groan, she flopped onto her back and stared at the digital clock on the oak nightstand—10:16 a.m. Okay, this was a ranch and she knew people had work to do but really, did they have to be so loud?

Her problem could be solved if she just got up and checked the windows. It seemed a simple fix until she tried to swing her legs off the side of the bed. They felt as if they weighed a hundred pounds each. So did her head. She wasn't the least hungover, even though it felt that way. After work she and Sadie'd had one lousy shot. That was it. And Nikki doubted she would've had anything to drink if Trace had come to the bar last night.

That got her heart pumping faster and her eyes fully open.

Okay, maybe she was coming out of a blackout because that was the stupidest thought ever. She glanced around her room, spotted her phone where she'd left it to charge on the massive dresser and forced her feet to the floor. She had to squint at the screen in order to focus on the date. Yep, it was Saturday. Last time she'd seen Trace was Thursday when the blonde had chased after him.

Come to think of it, Nikki hadn't seen the woman last night, either. Only the friend she'd come with two nights earlier. Which probably meant that she and Trace were…

No. She didn't care what Trace was doing. She didn't. Thinking about him at all would make her a fool. Or maybe it was a form of therapy…or avoidance…transference…something like that. She couldn't think about Trace and Wallace at the same time. If she tried, Trace won.

Sometimes she missed the rinky-dink Houston community college that had been close enough to work that she could walk.

She'd loved studying psychology until she learned how much schooling it took to actually get a useful degree. It could've been fun and challenging but she was nothing if not realistic. Higher education required money. And that was something she'd never have to spare.

She set the phone down, lingering to touch the smooth oak.

Matt said the hand-carved dresser had been in the family for over a hundred years. She wondered if that meant it was an antique. Or just old. She never could figure out the difference. One thing she knew for sure, the obnoxiously big mir-

ror mounted on the back was newer and really had to go if
she stayed much longer.

Staring at the dark smudges under her eyes because she'd
been too lazy to remove her makeup was not how she wanted
to wake up. Her hair was a mess. She'd worn it in a ponytail last night rather than iron out the two stubborn kinks
that had appeared as it dried on its own. And oh, yeah, they
were still there.

Hearing voices, she turned to the window. She'd meant
to close it when she got up. Now she could swear she heard
Trace.

But he wouldn't be here. He had too much to do at the Sundance, and besides, she doubted he'd step foot on Lone Wolf
property. Not as long as Wallace owned it.

She shoved the curtain aside and yanked the cord to raise
the closed blinds. Matt and Trace stood near the walkway
below, talking, but her impatience with the blinds drew their
attention.

Trace tipped his head back, and with his forefinger, pushed
up the brim of his Stetson. With the sun shining on his tanned
face, his green eyes seemed to sparkle. "Morning, sunshine,"
he said, his mouth curving in a grin.

Nikki knew exactly what she looked like and her first instinct was to jump back and jerk the curtain closed. But giving in would only tell him she cared how he saw her. And
that was so much worse. "God, can you be any louder? Some
of us have to work at night."

"Have to?" Matt lifted an eyebrow at her. Apparently he
wasn't in the best mood. He hated that she worked at the Watering Hole instead of adjusting to the ranch, though lately
he hadn't said much. "I'm pretty sure you could've gone to
sleep earlier than four."

Her heart sank. If he knew when she'd turned off her lamp,
that probably meant he'd been up with Wallace. In fact, Matt

looked drawn and tired. She was the worst sister in the whole world. How did he put up with her?

"Would y'all like some coffee?" Her neckline had slipped down her shoulder and she pulled the nightshirt back in place. "I'll bring it out to you."

"Sure." Matt rubbed his eyes, then frowned. "No, that's okay. I wasn't thinking... Go back to bed."

"I'm up. It's no trouble."

"I wouldn't mind a cup." Trace wasn't smiling anymore but he was staring up at her.

Her nightshirt was made of thin yellow T-shirt fabric and she wasn't wearing a bra. No, he wasn't being obvious or horrible but he'd noticed all right. "Cream and sugar?" she asked, stepping backward.

"I like my women sweet, my coffee not so much."

Nikki rolled her eyes and noticed Matt trying not to smile. "Is that your oh-so-charming way of saying no sugar?"

"You got it, darlin'."

She hated when he called her that, and he knew it. The smile was back, and he might've winked, she wasn't sure with the sun in his face. Very tempting to renege on the offer, go back to bed and let them get their own coffee. Oh, who was she kidding? She'd never go back to sleep knowing he was just outside. She only wished she knew why he was here.

"Okay, give me a few minutes." She pulled the curtain closed and grabbed a pair of jeans she'd tossed on the blue upholstered chair last night.

It took her a minute to sift through her underwear drawer before she realized he wouldn't actually see that her bra and panties matched. Sighing, she plucked a black thong from the pile along with the most unflattering white bra she owned. She found a clean red T-shirt, washed her face, brushed her teeth, then twisted her hair up and clipped it.

She hurried to the kitchen, still wondering what Trace was

doing here. All she needed was for him to flirt with her like he did at the bar. She didn't know how Matt would react. He liked Trace but Matt was protective of her and he'd seen how Trace behaved around the Sundance guests.

But then Trace already had kind of flirted with her earlier. Or maybe that was just how a guy teased his friend's kid sister. In many ways, having a brother was still new to her. Little things surprised her, like how Matt worried that she drove home alone at midnight. It was that sort of reaction that made her realize Matt didn't truly understand how she and her mom had lived. Because Nikki would feel a whole lot safer with a pack of coyotes than she'd felt in her old neighborhood.

Holding three mugs made it hard to open the front door. She managed, but pulling it closed was trickier. If only she had someplace to set down…

In seconds Trace was at her side. "I figured you went back to bed," he said, closing the door and reaching for a mug. "Which one's mine?"

"The blue." She held it out to him.

He wrapped his hand around the cup, his warm fingers brushing against her knuckles. It had to be deliberate, the way he let the tips trail along the backs of her own fingers before he took the mug from her.

She stared down at his hand. "You have calluses."

"What?" He gave her a funny look. "I work on a ranch, you know. Here, I'll take Matt's."

"I didn't mean anything. I was just—" She let go of the coffee with cream and sugar, and this time, he was careful not to touch her. "Trace?"

He'd already started walking toward Matt and acknowledged her with a quick glance over his shoulder.

It was too awkward to talk with all that space between them. Plus Matt would hear her fumbling to explain that the calluses had surprised her and she had no idea why. She followed him in mute frustration wishing Matt wasn't standing so close to the corral where two mean-looking horses had been kept yesterday. No sign of them now, but Nikki was already edgy and she preferred a vast distance between her and where any animal the size of a horse might be. Dogs and cats were fine. She'd always wanted a cocker spaniel or a cute little poodle. But people's fascination with horses? She didn't get it. Those beasts were huge and dangerous.

"You said something back there." Trace had already given Matt his coffee, and he was leaning against the railing watching her as she joined them. Well, sort of joined them…by stopping a good six feet away. "Sorry, I didn't catch it."

"Oh, it was nothing." She cradled her mug with both hands and sipped from it, sweeping a gaze toward the barn and stable.

"You haven't been out here before, have you?" Matt asked, and Trace laughed.

She could see why he thought it was a joke. They weren't *that* far from the walkway, but still farther than she'd ever ventured. The area between the front door and where she parked the truck on the side of the house, now that was her turf.

"No," she said, and had to clear her throat and try again. "I haven't."

A pair of hired hands left the barn on noisy ATVs so no one bothered to say anything. Trace drank his coffee, watching her, his brows puckered in a slight frown. She hoped he wouldn't ask why she hadn't been to the corral, because she didn't really want to answer in front of Matt. He didn't know about her fear of large animals. It had only started after she'd watched him compete in the Houston rodeo last year.

He was a professional bull rider, with fancy belt buckles and millions in prize money. Nothing intimidated him. He'd been calm and cool sitting on top of that fifteen-hundred-pound bull. She was pretty sure his eight-second ride had knocked a year off her life. That had been the first and last time she'd gone to a rodeo.

Matt kept glancing toward the stable as if he were waiting for someone. Trace apparently preferred to stare at her. It made her nervous, and she pretended not to notice, but what annoyed her most was that she would've liked the chance to check him out.

He wasn't dressed all that differently from when he came into the bar. If he owned more than one pair of pants that weren't jeans she'd be shocked. And he seemed to like T-shirts. He wore them all the time, even in this chilly morning air. Twice he'd come into the Watering Hole wearing cool Western-cut shirts. But the other guys gave him so much crap about it she knew it wasn't a normal thing. The cowboy boots and Stetson seemed to be daily requirements.

When the ATV engines had faded and they could be heard again, Matt spoke first. "Do you know if Wallace is awake?"

Nikki shrugged, feeling a bit defensive. No reason for it because Matt never criticized or pushed. He accepted her refusal to have anything to do with the man.

"How's he doing?" Trace asked.

Matt shrugged. "Depressed. Not even interested in drinking, if you can believe that."

"I believe it," Trace murmured.

"Yeah." Matt sighed. "Right." He knew Trace understood because his own father had died of cancer years ago. And Nikki knew this only because Matt had told her.

It got quiet after that. She wondered if Trace was thinking about his father. The McAllisters were a close family, but she didn't know anything about Trace's relationship with the man. Or much about Trace, really.

The night Matt had gotten beaten up was the only time she'd spent alone with Trace. She'd had a bit too much to

drink and he'd driven her home. He'd been a perfect gentle-
man, not even trying for a good-night kiss, though she knew
he really wanted to.

She wasn't used to guys like him. He'd kind of rattled her
at the time. But when she thought about it, all he'd really done
was show restraint. And only because she was Matt's sister.

Trace's mouth curved into a slow, sexy smile.

She blinked, her insides fluttering with the realization that
she'd been staring at him as if he were a hot fudge sundae.
And he was loving it.

"What are you doing here anyway?" she asked, wishing
she could just disappear. "Don't I see enough of you at the
Watering Hole? You have to come sniffing around here?"

"Jesus, Nikki." Matt frowned at her. "You need more sleep.
I phoned Trace. He's here to help me."

She looked from her brother to Trace, who was still smiling.

"It's true," he said, touching the brim of his hat. "Though
I'm always happy to see you, Nikki."

"Oh." She took another sip, sorry she'd gotten out of bed.
"So I'm interrupting."

"Nope." Trace casually glanced over his shoulder. "We're
just waiting."

"For who?"

"Petey," Matt said. "He's our best man, been here for over
twenty years. You met him yet?"

"Is he the really big guy with the shaggy beard?" she asked,
and when Matt nodded, she said, "I've seen him around but
I haven't actually met him. He always seems to be working
with the horses."

"That's what a wrangler does, though we can count on
Petey for just about anything."

"Nowadays we use ATVs a lot," Trace said. "Back when I
was a kid, everything was done on horseback and the horses

had to know how to work around the cattle. You needed a good wrangler so you didn't spend half your time with your ass planted in the dirt."

Matt nodded, grinning. "Now they even use helicopters for roundups and drives. The job's gotten too cushy."

"Hey, as soon as we start seeing profits again, we need to chip in, start a co-op and buy a chopper," Trace said. He put his mug on the corral post, then flexed his shoulders as if trying to get the stiffness out. "We've already got ourselves a pilot. That's half the battle, right?"

She knew he meant his brother Jesse, but she didn't understand the remark about profits. According to Matt the Lone Wolf was doing great. The Sundance seemed to be doing well, too. But watching Trace arch his back and stretch his arms in that snug black T-shirt, she couldn't concentrate on anything but his broad chest and muscular biceps. She'd never thought of him as the type to work out but he had to be lifting weights or something to account for the flat belly and ridges of muscle.

Trace straightened and let his arms fall to his sides, so she could finally relax. If he'd caught her staring she didn't know it because her gaze never made it higher than his chest.

She forced herself to look toward the barn where someone was moving out bales of hay. "What's that equipment called?"

They both looked, but Trace answered first. "It's just a Toolcat," he said. "Good for small jobs and tight places." Nikki felt a little guilty when she caught Matt's pleased expression. He thought she was finally showing interest in the place when all she really wanted was a distraction.

"Okay, here he comes." Matt's tone was all business, even his posture had changed as he peered toward the stable.

Trace turned his attention to Petey. He wasn't alone. The big grizzly looking man was leading the brown horse—the mean one from yesterday—toward them. As big as the wrangler was he seemed to be having trouble holding on to the animal when it reared up.

"He's a beauty," Trace murmured, slowly bending to slip between the wood railings into the corral.

Nikki tried to grab his arm and missed. "What are you doing?"

"Hey." Matt drew her back. "You have to be quiet."

After a brief struggle, Petey got the horse through the open gate. She watched in horror as Trace approached them from the opposite side. The horse put its head down low, arched its back and leaped into the air. Both men stepped clear as the animal came down on stiff legs.

Trace reached for the lead. "I got him," he said in a calm voice.

"God, Matt, don't let him do this," she whispered, her throat tight and raw. "Please."

"Trace knows what he's doing. Nobody's better with mustangs. But he doesn't need to be distracted. Understand?"

No, she didn't. How could she comprehend any of it? The horse's nostrils were flared and his eyes wild… He looked as if his mission was to kill Trace. She couldn't watch. If she'd had it in her power to make Trace leave the corral she would have.

She backed up slowly, covering her mouth because she didn't trust herself not to scream or do something equally stupid. All eyes were on the mustang, so she turned and ran to the house.

4

SHE'D BEEN SCARED to death. Trace had seen it in Nikki's flushed face and unfocused eyes, even the way her body had stiffened. What he didn't know was whether she was afraid of horses in general or this particular mustang. Trace had to admit, the stallion could be a mean-looking son of a bitch. But only because he'd been afraid, just like Nikki.

"You're feeling better now, aren't you, boy?" He wiped the powerful flank, lathered with sweat, and used the back of his free arm to blot his own wet forehead.

Stupid not to wear long sleeves. He should've known better.

The T-shirt was sticking to his sweaty body, so he pulled it off and used a dry spot to mop his face. He had a spare in his truck that probably ought to be tossed in the rag bin but it would serve the purpose until he got home.

After three hours, the mustang was exhausted, and so was Trace. Diablo was the most fiercely stubborn horse he'd gone up against in a long time. Since the stallion had been purchased only two days earlier, he hadn't actually been named yet. But Trace figured why not go for the obvious, the Spanish word for devil.

Matt walked out of the barn with a young hand and more

bottles of water. Trace had lost track of how many he'd gulped down just in the past hour alone. A drop of sweat trickled into his eye. He squeezed it closed and used the T-shirt to stop the sting. When he could open his eye again he looked toward the house and saw Nikki standing at her window.

She moved back, and he pretended he hadn't seen her. He wondered if Matt knew about her fear of horses. Trace didn't think so. If he did, it wouldn't be like Matt to let his sister come anywhere near an untamed mustang. It didn't matter that she hadn't been in danger. Seeing the stallion's wild-eyed look wouldn't win her over.

And her living on a ranch of all places? Man, no wonder she hightailed it off the Lone Wolf every chance she got. Matt had mentioned he thought her skittishness was about Wallace. Since she obviously hadn't spoken up about her phobia, Trace wouldn't say a word, either. Not to Matt, anyway. But he fully intended on having a talk with Nikki. She'd never give the Lone Wolf a shot if she didn't figure out that a horse was harmless if you treated it right. And Matt really wanted his sister to stay.

Truthfully, Trace wouldn't mind, either. Hell, if he really wanted to be honest, he'd outright admit he wanted her to stick around. Admit it to himself, anyway. No one else needed to know he was getting a little soft.

Diablo sure knew. Reading Trace's sudden energy shift like a book, the stallion tossed his head and stamped the ground. Rotten timing. Matt and the hand had just reached them, and the poor kid looked as if he might pee his jeans.

"He's okay," Trace said, stroking the mustang's neck. "It was me. I got him a little jumpy. I'll take him back to the stable and give him a good brushing. All will be forgiven."

"No, you won't," Matt said. "You've worked hard enough. Lester is gonna take him." Matt passed Trace a water. "I got beer inside if you want."

Holding on to the lead, Trace eyed the young man. "You're Morgan's boy, aren't you?"

"Yes, sir. I'm the oldest."

"I thought you were still in high school."

"Graduated last month."

"Sorry," Matt said. "I figured you guys knew each other. Things have changed in the ten years since I moved away."

"Not so much." Trace held out the lead, which Lester seemed reluctant to take. "I doubt he'll give you trouble. Just stay calm, keep your voice low." Trace let go once he saw the boy had him. To Matt, he said, "By the way, I think this one needs to be called Diablo."

Lester groaned. "Great."

Matt and Trace both laughed.

Trace clapped the kid on the shoulder as he turned slowly toward the stable. "Son, I wouldn't let you take him if I thought he'd be too rowdy for you." He watched Lester and Diablo move toward the stable, then caught Matt staring at him. "What?"

"Son?" Matt chuckled. "He's what…seventeen? You've got only ten years on that kid."

"You have been away too long. Hell, I call Jesse son and he's five years older than me." Trace downed more water but kept his gaze on the boy and the mustang. He wasn't necessarily worried, but it didn't hurt to be cautious. If he had to make a dash, he was ready. "You remember Lester's father, right?"

"You said Morgan?" Matt frowned, shaking his head. "To tell you the truth, I've been so busy with Wallace and straightening out payroll, I don't even know all the men who live in the bunkhouse, much less the day hands. Duke is still the foreman. He's been running things."

"Morgan Dunn was a year ahead of Cole in school. He stepped in as quarterback at the last minute and took us to finals."

Matt swung a stunned look at Lester's retreating back. "That Morgan? He has a son that age?"

"He knocked up his girlfriend senior year. They're still married and running her dad's ranch. It's a small operation but they haven't gone under and that's something." Trace rolled his left shoulder. It was getting stiff again and he was tired of the sun beating down on him. He often worked without a shirt when he was mending fences but not at this time of day. He started for the gate, and Matt walked along with him.

"Man, do I feel old."

"You are old."

"Thanks." Matt snorted. "Tell your sister she'd better hurry and marry me while I can still get it up."

"Nah, she's gotta wait for Cole to tie the knot with Jamie, then Jesse has to marry Shea. It's a McAllister tradition. Oldest to youngest. Everyone's gotta wait their turn."

Matt stopped and gave him a panicked look.

Trace laughed, scooped up the mug he'd left on the railing and looked at Matt. His expression hadn't changed. "Tell me you aren't that damn gullible."

"You're older than Rachel," Matt said with a straight face. "That's gonna be a long wait. Who the hell would marry you?"

Trace automatically glanced up at Nikki's window. He didn't know why. She wasn't there, but that didn't matter. That he'd looked was stupid.

Matt started them walking again. "Yeah, good luck with that."

"What?"

Matt just smiled, then nodded at the T-shirt Trace had balled in his hand. "I owe you a shirt."

"I'm not messing around with your sister." Trace kept his eyes on the ground. He'd never been more confused over a woman in his life. No matter what he tried, he couldn't seem to get her out of his head. Staying away from the Watering Hole hadn't helped. The only thing he knew for sure was that if he made a move, he'd better be serious about her. Matt was a friend and soon he'd be family. "I know better."

"Hey, not my business. Nikki's a big girl, and she knows her own mind. If she doesn't want you messing with her, she won't be shy about letting you know." Matt grinned. "If I need to worry, it should be about you. Cross her and she'll chew you up and spit you out."

"Yeah. I can see that." Trace laughed, because that's what Matt expected, but he wondered if Matt really believed his own words. Nikki might not be as tough as he thought.

But then Trace was starting to get the feeling she was a little mixed up about how tough she was, too. It wasn't just about her being afraid of horses. She'd told him about the gang violence in her old neighborhood, so he understood she'd needed to come off hard as nails. That didn't mean she hadn't been scared a time or two. She liked to pretend nothing bothered her. But he'd seen her feeling defenseless and uncertain, and trying her damnedest to hide it.

Maybe that tug-of-war between vulnerability and bravery had gotten to him, because something sure was preventing him from keeping his distance. He wasn't the kind of guy who needed to ride to the rescue, either. Still, for her to live on a ranch and fear horses? That was unnecessary grief. Maybe he could help her with that.

They were approaching the house. Trace's truck was parked over on the right. "You want to come in for that beer?" Matt asked. "I just need to check on Wallace first."

"No, I got a lot to do at the Sundance yet. I'm just gonna give this mug to Nikki."

"I can take it…" Matt's voice trailed off. "Sure, come on in."

"I'm too grimy. Mind asking her to meet me at the door?"

"Just wipe your boots so Lucy won't take a broom to both of us, but otherwise you're fine to come inside." Matt opened the door while scraping off his own boots. "I'll call her. She's probably in her room." He stuck out his hand and they shook. "Thanks. I appreciate what you did with Diablo."

"Anytime." Trace looked around. "It was good seeing how well kept the place is."

A loud kitchen noise had Matt frowning over his shoulder. "I'll go get her. See you soon, huh?"

Trace nodded, waited until Matt left and then used the rest of the water and his T-shirt to wipe his face and upper body. He figured he had time to run to his truck for the other shirt, but he'd taken only one step off the porch when he heard Nikki.

"Everything okay?" she asked, her voice at a nervous pitch.

"Sure." He turned to her. "Just fine," he said, smiling. But she didn't see because her gaze was aimed at his bare chest. "Sorry. I was just about to get a clean shirt out of my truck."

"Huh?" Her eyes slowly lifted to meet his. "Oh, no problem. Matt said you wanted to see me?"

Trace had to quietly clear his throat. No mistaking the look on her face. She liked what she saw. "I wanted to give you this." He stepped back up onto the porch, holding out the mug.

"Oh." She took it from him. "Did you want more coffee?"

"No, but I'd like you to come for a short walk with me."

"Where?"

"To the stable."

Her eyes widened. "Why?"

"You don't have to get close to the horses." Trace made sure his hand was clean, then held it out to her. He'd been sensitive about the calluses earlier but he got it. Nikki had only seen him as goodwill ambassador to the guests. Maybe it was time for her to see that he worked on the ranch just like any other man. She might not like it but he was a cowboy.

She stared at his palm, then up at him. "You didn't answer me."

"I want to show off Diablo. He's much better behaved now."

She let out a laugh. "Diablo?"

Trace smiled. "I don't know what Matt's going to call him. Until an hour ago the name seemed appropriate. Are you gonna leave me standing here with my hand out?"

Sighing, her gaze slid to his outstretched palm, then to his chest.

"Don't worry. I'll put a shirt on first."

"I'm not worried about that." She clutched the mug so tightly he hoped she didn't break it.

Maybe he was wrong to push her. Maybe he needed to let her take more time to get used to the Lone Wolf. He withdrew his hand and stuffed it in his front pocket. "That's okay, Nikki," he said, stepping back. "I should get going, anyway."

"Are all the horses in their stalls?" she asked in a rush.

"They are." He paused, knowing he had no business making that assumption. Lester could've brought one out to groom. "I'll make sure they are before you go inside."

She studied his face, as if trying to decide if she should trust him. "Let me get rid of this," she said, waving the mug. "Want me to take that water bottle, too?"

"Thanks." He passed it to her. "Seems you're always waiting on me. We ever get over to Kalispell, I'll have to buy you dinner."

Her lips parted and she darted another look at his chest.

For a second he got excited that she might be interested in going on that drive, then just as quickly regretted mentioning Kalispell again so soon. Though she didn't tell him to get lost, just went back into the house with the mug and bottle, even left the door open a little so that was a good sign she'd come back.

Skipping the steps, he jumped off the porch and hurried to his truck. If he remembered correctly, the white T-shirt had a small stain and the hem was frayed but it would do. He found it wadded up on the backseat, shook it out and sniffed the armpit area just to be sure. Yeah, it was clean enough.

He pulled the shirt over his head, stuck his arms in the sleeves, tugged down the hem and heard the seam tear. He looked down. It wasn't just the seam but a large hole in the front. "Well, shit."

Muffled laughter brought his head up. Watching him from the porch, Nikki tilted her head to the side. "I hadn't seen that style yet. It's a good look for you."

"Hell, I don't care. I'd wear it like this if I were headed home."

She shrugged. "Wear it now. I don't care, either." She frowned slightly. "Or go without a shirt," she said, and averted her eyes.

He hid his smile by yanking the T-shirt off. She could shrug and toss her hair as though she was indifferent all she wanted. Right now she was so easy to read it almost felt as if he was cheating. "I bet Matt would lend me one."

She turned so sharply to him, her ponytail whipped to the side. "Can we just go and get this over with?"

"We can." He got rid of the shirt and closed the truck door. "Try not to be jumpy. Animals can sense your mood."

"Well, great because—" She shoved her hands deep into the pockets of her jeans and stared down at her track shoes. "You know, don't you?"

They started to walk. "I'm not sure what you mean," he said, his gaze snagging on her slender neck.

"That I'm afraid."

"I suspected. Is it only horses?"

She kept her head down. "Bulls. I hate bulls, too. I saw

Matt ride once… Never again. I wish he'd quit the circuit and stay here."

"That's the plan, isn't it?"

"No, I mean, quit right now. He's scheduled for five or six more events this year."

"I'm pretty sure Rachel feels like you do. Bull riding can be a dangerous—" Trace cut himself off. It was too late. He saw her shoulders tense. What the hell was wrong with him? "Matt is good. And he's careful. He's got you and Rachel in his life now. He'll finish his career in one piece."

"I hope so," she murmured, hunching her shoulders forward and sounding small and fretful.

Trace slipped his hand around her nape. She shot him a startled look, but he just smiled, left his hand right there and massaged her tense muscles as they continued to walk.

She moved a little closer to him, which kicked his heart rate up. He kept kneading and rubbing her soft warm skin and by the time they reached the stable, she'd started to relax. They hadn't made it inside yet when one of the horses whickered and she went stiff again. She stopped, probably would've jerked away if he hadn't been caressing the back of her neck. The pulse below her jaw beat wildly.

"Wait right here, okay?" Trace moved his hand to her chin and urged her to look up at him. "I'm going to make sure Lester is done brushing Diablo."

"Who?"

"He's a kid who works here."

She stayed motionless, only her eyes moved to sweep a gaze inside the dim stable.

Trace didn't want to let go. He'd give just about anything to let his fingers trail down to her collarbone, slip beneath the scooped neckline. Just a little…he only wanted to feel more skin. Hell, he wanted more than that, but for now, what he cared about most was for her not to be afraid.

"Nikki?" He waited for her to look at him. Her eyes were black and filled with so much fear it sliced into his confidence. Maybe this wasn't the right thing to do. He was good with horses. Everyone assumed he was good with women. And mostly he was…flirting was easy. But he'd never been tested when it really counted. "Can you trust me? I'm not going to let anything happen to you."

She stared into his eyes and moistened her lips. Taking in a deep breath, she lifted her hand, and he expected her to push him away. She held on to his wrist. "No offense. I don't trust anyone."

Trace smiled. That wasn't entirely true but if that's what she wanted to believe…

Her grip on his wrist tightened. "Does Matt know?"

"Not from me."

"Whatever happens in there, don't tell him."

Now he knew he'd screwed up. Lester was inside. The kid might talk. "I won't say a word. Will you wait here? I'll be right back."

She nodded, her gaze still locked with his, and he wanted to kiss her. Right here, where the sunlight glistened off those soft full lips and glowed from her golden skin. Fear slowly faded from her eyes replaced by something that looked suspiciously like it could be trust. Whatever it was it stopped his foolish thoughts and he let her go before his good sense ended up in the dust.

NIKKI WATCHED TRACE disappear into the cavernous stable. Along with him went her short-lived confidence. That she couldn't fully appreciate the breadth of his shoulders or the muscular definition of his back told her how out of control her fear had grown. Back at the porch when she couldn't smell and hear the animals, she'd been real clear that she wanted him with his shirt off. Now all she could think about was whether or not to run.

He wouldn't force her to get too close to the horses, and even if he tried she'd refuse. But what if being in a stable made everything worse? Oh, she really did believe Trace wouldn't let any harm come to her, but she also believed that the horses could sense she was terrified. If facing her terror head-on didn't work, it would be murder living on the Lone Wolf. Maybe she could find an apartment in town. Sadie would know…

From deep inside the stable someone was walking toward her. Not Trace, but a shorter, huskier guy. He was young, she saw when he stepped out of the shadows, his hair lighter. Had to be the guy Trace mentioned. Already she'd forgotten his name.

"Hi," he said as he got closer, eyeing her with curiosity.

"Hey." She hugged herself, doing her share of sizing him up as he passed, checking for signs of evil-horse attack.

She casually angled to her left to inspect him from the back. His clothes weren't torn and there was no blood. He wasn't limping. All good to know.

"Nikki?"

She must've jumped three feet in the air before she spun toward Trace. "God, scare the hell out of me, why don't you?"

He raised both hands, palms out. "Sorry."

Okay, for the moment she could appreciate his chest. It was mostly smooth, just a faint dusting of hair between his brown nipples.

"You ready?"

"I guess." She sucked in as much air as she could manage and wiped her damp palms down the front of her jeans.

"Good. Keep taking deep breaths."

"If I tell you I have to leave then I'm leaving. Period."

"Got it."

"It does not mean I'm opening the subject for negotiation."

"Glad you cleared that up."

She swung a look at him. "I'm serious."

"Me, too. You women seem to think everything requires a discussion."

Nikki gaped at him, then noticed they'd advanced several feet inside. Bales of hay were stacked in the corner. On a railing three saddles sat in a row. The scent of leather and weirdly, soap, was strong. "Are you purposely being an ass to distract me?"

"Think about it. You ask a guy if he wants to stop for a drink, and he says yes or no. A man asks a woman the same question and what does he get?— 'Oh, I don't know, isn't it too late? What do you think?'" He'd raised his pitch to mimic a feminine voice and Nikki almost laughed.

"That's not true," she said. "And it's sexist."

He finger-combed back his dark hair, and frowned as if giving the matter serious thought. "You're probably right about it being sexist, but I swear to God it's true."

"Really? Ask me again about going to Kalispell and see what I have to say."

Trace grinned and caught her hand. "I wish we were at the Sundance. Then I'd know all the horses' names."

She slowly looked to her left. They were standing in front of the first stall, but she didn't remember walking this far in.

The horse looked at her with its ears pricked forward.

Nikki moved closer to Trace. "Is it male or female?"

"She's a mare. You might hear someone refer to her as a roan. That's for the color. The paint over there might be referred to as a pinto."

"I won't touch her," Nikki said, watching the mare's nose strain over the stall door. "Any of them."

"I wouldn't let you. I don't know these horses. We're just

having a look." He slid his arm around her shoulders and she leaned into him as they kept walking.

Despite the fact that he'd been working in the sun and sweating, he smelled nice. Very masculine. Very different. Whatever combination made up his scent it was a turn-on. She almost forgot they were surrounded by horses. For a second she considered sliding her arm around his waist but didn't. It would be crazy to let this turn into something else. This was perfect. She had an excuse for the clammy palms and racing heart. No need for Trace to know he was partly responsible. The fiery tingle low in her belly was all him.

He rubbed her arm. "Maybe some day when you're at the Sundance helping Rachel and Jamie I'll take you to our stable."

"You're never there when I am." She bit her lip, wishing she hadn't admitted she'd noticed his absence.

"I figured you were trying to avoid me."

"I only go over to cover for Rachel when she's busy with Matt or if Jamie calls."

"Ah. I won't take it personally then."

She didn't have to look to know he was grinning. She much preferred keeping her eye on the stalls as they walked by. A horse at the back made an angry sound. "Gee, don't tell me…that's Diablo."

"He's still getting used to being penned in."

"Maybe we should turn around."

"You've trusted me this far. Give me five minutes. You can stand as far back as you want."

"The next county?" She sighed. "Five minutes." Neither of them wore a watch. So what? She'd know when it was time to make a run for it.

They got to the last stall, and Trace took his arm from around her shoulders. She moved back as he stood at the stall and stroked the horse's neck.

"Mustangs have a reputation for being harder to tame and train than other breeds. They're innately suspicious of humans."

"So he was wild when Matt bought him?"

"Someone else had him for a short while, but they couldn't handle him."

It had taken Trace about three hours. She'd watched him from her window, awed by his patience, never speaking above a whisper. The horse had responded fairly quickly all things considered.

"See this black hair rimming his ear? We call them black points." Trace stayed focused on the stallion, murmuring things she couldn't hear. She was beginning to think he'd forgotten about her when he said, "I have a proposition for you, Nikki."

"What's that?" she asked, suspicious when his gaze remained on the horse.

"Let me teach you to ride."

"Diablo?"

"No." The corners of his mouth quirked, but he kept the smile in check. "I have a Sundance mare in mind."

She didn't care if it was a pony. "Why? What's the point?"

"You live on a ranch. It'll be easier when you see you have nothing to fear."

"I've been doing just fine by staying in my own corner."

"You're also missing out. Horses are terrific animals." Trace met her eyes. "Come on, Nikki, give me a shot."

Breathing in deeply, she turned her gaze to the stallion, and watched Trace stroke its velvety neck. "Okay," she said, the word nearly sticking in her throat. She hated feeling afraid... of anything.

5

THE NEXT DAY Trace waited for Nikki at the agreed upon spot, a grassy field between the Lone Wolf and the Sundance. It was the perfect place because she could easily access it by truck, and yet they'd have privacy.

He'd brought Gypsy, a sweet bay mare that was a guest favorite because of her gentle disposition. She rarely spooked and she was also on the small side, a good size for Nikki to control. Not that he expected her to climb in the saddle right away. She had to get to know Gypsy first and let confidence squeeze out some of the fear.

Damn, he hoped she hadn't changed her mind. He glanced at his watch. She was only five minutes late. Nothing to sweat over. He thought he'd given her good directions but he might've taken a turn or two for granted. There weren't many landmarks out here.

He checked his phone to make sure she hadn't called him to cancel, relieved to see he didn't have a voice mail. It wouldn't have shocked him if she'd had second thoughts, but she wouldn't leave him dangling. A moment later he heard the truck, and through the aspens and spruces, saw flashes of chrome reflecting the sunlight.

Gypsy barely reacted. The mare was used to the sound of

vehicles around the Sundance, but he stroked her neck, passing his calm energy to her. Then Nikki parked and climbed out of the truck in tight jeans and there went his composure. He was still fine on the outside, it was just his pulse that seemed to be headed for a finish line. Gypsy danced a bit to the side, but he held on to the reins and hoped Nikki hadn't seen the nervous step.

She walked toward him, her gaze fixed on the mare, her hands restless until she buried them in her front pockets. "Hey."

"You have any trouble finding the road?"

"Only one wrong turn." She finally met his eyes. "FYI, it's not a road."

He smiled. "It's gotten overgrown since I was here last. Gypsy and I rode over the grass a few times to make a trail for you."

"She's a bay," Nikki said, stopping a fair distance away and eyeing the mare as if she were an opponent in a boxing match. "I did some checking online so I'd know what I was getting myself into."

"Good for you doing your own research. The more you know what to expect, the better." He could stare at her sexy pink mouth and almond-shaped eyes all day, so he turned back to Gypsy before he forgot what he was supposed to be doing. "She's about the best tempered horse I know. Josh and I use her to give riding lessons to the guests. Come closer. She wants to meet you."

Nikki seemed to favor close-fitting stretchy shirts with necklines that dipped just low enough to make a man itch. He'd seen her wear four different colors. Today's was yellow. And with the deep breaths she was taking, he'd have to watch himself. It didn't help that he'd spent too long in the shower wondering how those lips would feel....

"I have to admit, she does have a sweet face." Nikki stepped closer. "You're holding on to her, right?"

"I am. Honestly I don't need to, but we're gonna take our time, let you two get acquainted for a while."

She nodded, eyes only for Gypsy. "I'm not sure what I'm supposed to do."

"As soon as you're comfortable, you keep moving closer. Remember what I told you yesterday about a horse's ears?"

"Yes, forward means friendly or curious. And I'm trying to keep my voice quiet and even."

Trace smiled. "You're doing fine."

"Oh, the other thing I read was that quarter horses are good horses to use to teach someone to ride."

"That's partly true, I suppose, but more important, the horse should be used to beginners. Also important is that I know the horse well." He pulled off his right glove. "You can get online and read for hours, but it comes down to whether you trust me or not."

Her lips parted and she tore her gaze away from the mare to look at him. "I do," she said softly.

They were only talking about a horse and riding lessons, for Christ's sake. No reason for his chest to tighten. "Good." Obviously he'd been looking into those pretty brown eyes too long. He switched his focus to Gypsy. "Makes it easier all the way around."

"I'm coming closer now."

He didn't want to make her more nervous by watching her inch forward, but he'd never met anyone this scared of a horse before. She wasn't faking like some of the guests had done to get his attention. Her face was pale and if he touched her hand he'd bet it would be ice-cold. She stopped after three steps.

"Nikki?" He moved away from Gypsy to get closer to Nikki, but the mare went with him making her retreat. "Sorry. My fault." He tethered Gypsy to a shrub, then went to Nikki.

Her eyes locked on the loose tie. "Will that hold her?"

"She'll stay right where she is. That really was my fault." He pulled off his other glove before he reached for her. "What are you afraid will happen?"

"I—I'm not sure." She frowned at his fingers wrapping around her upper arm. His thumb almost touched his middle finger. The sassy mouth and tempting curves made him forget how small she really was.

"I'm not going to force you to do anything, so you can relax."

She smiled a little. "You're treating me like Diablo. Letting me get used to your touch."

"Something like that."

Her lashes lifted and her eyes looked every bit as enticing as her body. "Why?"

"So we can approach Gypsy together." He put an arm around her shoulders, and held her against his side. And then ordered himself to calm the hell down. Finding out he was getting hard wouldn't ease her mind.

"Okay," she said, her body stiff.

"You're short. I think you're afraid the horse might lunge forward and overpower you."

"Maybe. Yeah."

"I still have a free hand to block her, but it won't be necessary. Think this might help?" he asked, feeling her start to relax. "Two to one, plus I'm taller than Gypsy."

"I was thinking a stool, but yes, this—"

The mare stepped closer. Nikki grabbed his hand and pulled his arm across her middle like a shield. Leaning into his side she tried to move them backward.

"You're okay," he said, his arms circling her protectively. Not wanting to lose ground, he slipped behind her, holding her against his chest, ignoring her death grip on his forearm. "Gypsy was probably curious, that's all."

She nodded, her gaze trained on the mare, her fingers digging deeper into his muscle. Her hair smelled like a beach drink, something with coconut and vanilla in it. The soft shiny strands caught on his roughened chin, though he'd shaved early this morning. He should've been more thoughtful and waited until just before he came to meet her. Taking another pleasant whiff, he vaguely reasoned that needing a razor didn't play into any part of today's—

Shit.

He froze in sheer panic, though he obviously wasn't panicked enough. She was too short for her ass to be a strategic hit to his fly, but her lower back was doing a fine job. He had an erection the size of a national monument.

"Hey, you know…" He moved so that they weren't touching, caught her shoulders when she lost her footing. "A stool is a good idea." He couldn't let her turn around and see him like this, let her think his motives for bringing her out here were anything but aboveboard. "I'll get one and you can keep it in your truck for next time."

Dammit all to hell. He rushed past her, afraid there wasn't enough cold water in the whole state of Montana to cool him down.

"Trace." Nikki understood the problem. What she didn't know was whether she should admit it or try to act as if she hadn't noticed. If she came clean, she risked the chance that this innocent and very sweet overture on Trace's part would turn into something that couldn't be undone. Because she was turned on, too. How could she not be?

She knew what was under that brown T-shirt. And he had strong muscled arms that made her feel protected and safe—which was juvenile, because she knew better, from personal experience. A man could use his good looks and charm to make a woman believe promises he had no intention of honoring.

To be fair to Trace, he was slowly proving that maybe she'd been too quick to judge him. He had sides to him she hadn't expected. In his own subtle way, Matt had tried to tell her there was more to Trace. But as much as she had grown to love her brother, when it came to men, she trusted her own instincts over anyone else's. Right now, though, she was a little shaky in that department.

"Trace."

"Yep." He was keeping his back to her and stroking Gypsy's neck.

Nikki had no desire to get in the mare's space or to embarrass him, so she stayed back a few feet. "Thank you for taking time away from your work to do this for me. Gypsy, I want to thank you, too."

He smiled at her over his shoulder, then frowned and leaned into the mare, his ear close to her muzzle. "What's that?" He drew back, looking annoyed and glaring at poor Gypsy. "I've warned you about your manners."

Nikki laughed. "Okay... What did she say?"

"'Talk is cheap. Where's my damn apple.'"

"You're nuts."

"Yeah, Gypsy said that, too." He was still smiling when he moved to unfasten the saddlebag.

She knew he couldn't still be hard or he'd be turned away, but she had to look. Not quite normal yet, though not nearly as impressive as five minutes ago. She almost sighed. Such a waste.

Gypsy had to know what was coming. Stretching her neck, she turned to watch him pull out her treat.

"I'm not sure why, but I'm surprised you feed her apples."

"I don't usually." He shrugged. "Sometimes I let a guest give her one. I thought you might like to."

"Um, I—I—" She ended in a soft whimper.

"Not now. I'd hoped we'd get a little further." He gave the glossy red apple to Gypsy, who chomped down on it. Wow, she had big teeth. "Maybe next time," he said. "You still game to try again?"

"Tomorrow?"

He shook his head. "Maybe the day after. I've got something going on in the morning and can't predict when I'll be done."

She'd bet it had something to do with the guests, which shouldn't matter to her. And it didn't...not at all...

Now that she thought about it, he hadn't flirted with her once. Not like he did at the bar. The hard-on didn't count. It was a natural physical reaction and he'd run from it.

Huh.

"You know I don't have to leave yet," she said. "Unless you do."

"No, I planned on us spending a couple hours out here. What time do you have to be at Sadie's?"

"Around five."

"You going straight there?"

She nodded. "I'm not hot and sweaty so I don't need to go home first."

He gazed up at the passing cloud cover, adjusting his hat to protect his eyes. "It feels nice in the shade."

"Yes, it does."

Silence stretched, and she didn't understand why it suddenly seemed awkward between them. They'd moved past the embarrassing hard-on thing easily. Was he disappointed that she hadn't made much progress with Gypsy? She really had, she thought, staring at the mare who seemed to be looking for another snack. Standing here with no wall separating her and the horse was progress. And she hadn't had a single moment of pure dread, imagining evil lurking behind Gypsy's soft chocolate-brown eyes. Maybe she should explain that to him.

"I meant to—"

"This is the—"

They looked at each other, not smiling, just staring. It figured they'd both speak at once. And now nothing.

"I'll go first," Trace said. "I want to get it off my chest. If I overstepped earlier, I'm sorry."

"You didn't. It never crossed my mind that you had. Here I'm worrying that I disappointed you."

"What?" His brows rose in disbelief. "You're doing great. Ever think you'd get this close to a horse outside of a stall or corral?"

Nikki smiled. "I was going to point that out to you."

"Don't you worry, darlin', I'm paying attention."

Her mood deflated. "I really don't like you calling me that." She watched him frown and fidget with the brim of his Stetson. He called guests darlin' all the time. Especially if he'd forgotten the woman's name. She wouldn't explain why it bothered her. But she refused to be part of the herd. He could figure it out for himself. Or not. As long as he stopped.

"I won't do it anymore."

"Okay, then we're good." She patted her pockets for her keys, then remembered she'd left them in the ignition.

"If you're feeling edgy because of Wallace, we can wait on your lessons."

"I don't give a damn about the man, and you know it." That he would say something so stupid pissed her off. Why was everyone trying to make her feel guilty for not caring? She had no reason to feel anything but contempt.

"Doesn't matter if you care or not. He's sick and dying right there in the house. The atmosphere changes. For everyone." He kept looking at her, even when she glared back. "I bet the hands living in the bunkhouse who can't stand him are affected. That's the way it goes."

"What do you know about it?"

"It's been twelve years but I damn well remember what it was like when my dad died."

"No, you don't understand. Everyone loved your dad." Nikki regretted her childish tone the second she heard her own voice. But Trace didn't get it. People spoke Gavin McAllister's name with reverence.

"He was a great man. The best man I've ever known," Trace said, turning to pet Gypsy. "He was a fair employer. And a good father, though I might've argued that point a few times when I was fourteen and getting grounded every month." He smiled a little. "But to say everyone loved him? That's stretching it. Dad had some zero-tolerance rules about conduct on the ranch and if the line got crossed, there were no exceptions. Some guys didn't see that as being fair. He'd had his share of getting flipped off behind his back. But once my dad was too sick to get out and work alongside the men, the whole mood around the place changed.

"Even my friends didn't want to come over and play pool. For months Dad was confined to his bed, so nobody saw him. Just the family and the nurse who'd come out to check on him and bring pain meds. It's not only about knowing he's upstairs suffering, but looking around while you do everyday things and recognizing his absence. Lucy's feeling it, so is Matt, I guarantee you. And that's bound to affect you."

Nikki hadn't realized he'd switched from talking about his father to Wallace. She'd been too unsettled by the rawness in his voice and how his face had changed. Usually she was good at reading people. For all the gang-related funerals she'd attended, maybe she'd never seen loss up close, because right now, it felt as if she were staring it in the face. But after twelve years?

She was lucky she hated Wallace. If this is what loving and losing someone did to a person…

"Hey, I didn't mean to freak you out." Trace was back to being himself, but with a concerned frown aimed at her.

"You didn't."

"I'm trying to tell you that you don't have to act tough around me, Nikki. I get it."

"Act tough?" She scoffed. "I am tough. I've had to be. And no, you don't get it." She felt badly he'd spent those past few moments reliving his father's illness. She did. But their situations were different and she didn't like him thinking she was weak and needy.

"For the sake of argument, how about we agree that you can use me as a sounding board or a shoulder to cry on if the need arises."

"Look, I'm sorry about your dad. You have such a great family and he was too young, but I'm fine. I am. I—" She totally lost her train of thought when she saw tenderness soften the lines bracketing his mouth. Why did she find it so hard to accept kindness? She didn't doubt Trace's sincerity, so why was she always unprepared for it? Looking past him, she stared at the cloudless blue sky, the snowcapped peaks of the Rockies. So much beauty. She should be finding peace inside, not panic, certainly not fear that her legs would give out. Oh, God…

Trace was quick, startling both the mare and her. He reached Nikki, and put his arms around her before she could tell him to stop. She was tempted to sag against his broad chest until the shakiness passed. For that same reason, she struggled to get away from him. Maybe that was the trouble with him. He made her weak. His kindness, the concerned looks and gentle touches chipped away at her defenses. Some- how he seemed to see past her facade and that was dangerous for her. How had he even known about her horse phobia? Matt hadn't seen it.

"Come on, now. I'm not hurting you." Trace loosened his hold. "I'm not even gonna kiss you." He had that damn smile in his voice. "Of course if you want me to…"

She'd quit fighting him when he mentioned the kiss, but realized it only now. And then told herself it was better that she stay where she was so he couldn't see her face. "Trace, I swear—"

"I'm just teasing you." His short husky laugh skipped along her nerve endings. He began gently stroking her back, she imagined, much like how he'd been stroking Gypsy's neck. "I have something to say but not while we're looking at each other." He rested his chin on top of her head. His heart pounded against the palm she laid on his chest. "Okay?"

It was probably a trick to spark her curiosity. "I don't like my hands and arms trapped like this."

"Put them around my waist. I don't mind."

She laughed. "Oh, Trace."

"What?" He leaned back to look at her. "I'm serious. I have something to tell you."

"All right. I'm listening." She couldn't seem to stay mad at him, which was irritating in itself. Another reason she should stay away from him, not be meeting him in secret. If there was another guy like him on the planet, she sure hadn't met him.

His chest expanded on a sigh. "I've never told anyone this so I'd appreciate you not repeating it."

"I won't." She slipped her arms free and slid them around him, pressing her cheek to his chest, feeling his strong steady heartbeat.

"One day my father and I were mending fences in the north pasture. I was pissed off that I had to work that particular afternoon because we were having a dance at school later, and any one of the hands could've been doing the work.

But my dad, he had this thing about doing different projects with each son. Cole had had lots of one-on-one time with him when he was in high school and so had Jesse. Dad wanted to make sure we boys knew how to do everything on the ranch and felt it was a good way to spend individual time with us.

"Well, I bitched and moaned that I wouldn't be ready in time to pick up my date, it was my first dance and I'd be too tired to enjoy it and on and on. Normally he would've let me go and we would've rescheduled. But I'd done that to him twice before so I could try out for varsity football. Then once he'd had to cancel." Trace paused. "I reminded him of that and accused him of never having been that stubborn with Cole and Jesse. Not the day of their first dance. Why poor me?"

His sudden slide to sarcasm jolted her. She tried not to tense, especially since he was already holding her kind of tight, but she knew something bad was coming.

"He smiled at me, said 'you're right, son, this can wait for another time.' He looked tired and there was no reason for him to work alone. I told him he should ride back to the house with me. He shook his head, told me to go, and I was still mad, checking my watch and my phone, too anxious to jump in the shower to care what he did.

"The next day, he and my mom sat all of us kids down. Jesse was home for the weekend from college. And they told us Dad had cancer. He'd taken too long to go see the doc. The late diagnosis meant he didn't have much time left." Trace swallowed. "We never did finish the fence line together. That afternoon in the north pasture was the last day he got his hands dirty. When he'd said there'd be another time, he'd lied. He knew he was too weak. He'd wanted to give me that last day and I was a total friggin' self-centered asshole."

"Oh, God, Trace, don't—" She tried to look at him but he wouldn't let her. Unsure what emotion she'd find in his face, she let him have his dignity and just hugged him. "I hope you're not still holding on to that argument. From what I've heard about your dad, he would never want that for you."

"Wanna know what I regret the most? I never brought it up. It ate at me yet I pretended the argument never happened. Hell, it wasn't an argument, it was me mouthing off. I was so ashamed and stupid. That damn McAllister pride that kept him from seeing the doctor kept me from telling him I—" His voice broke. "Talk about stupid. I don't know why I'm telling you this."

Nikki knew why. He'd given her a piece of himself so she'd feel comfortable confiding in him. What an incredible gift. Her eyes were moist, and she blinked like crazy when he leaned back, threading his fingers through her hair. She finally looked up at him, and found his tender smile almost more than she could take.

"Thank you," she whispered.

"I didn't do anything."

She just smiled back, amazed at how familiar his face had become. His green eyes had darkened and his mouth looked firm and soft at the same time. "I don't suppose one kiss would hurt," she said, her heart pounding. "Do you?"

His brief hesitation surprised her, then he slowly lowered his head, and she pushed up onto her toes to meet him half-way.

6

HE SLANTED HIS MOUTH to fit hers better, and flipped the hat off his head when it got in the way. A soft kiss, a few nibbles, teasing her lips before he ran his tongue along the lower one. She opened for him, eager to taste him, anxious for him to give her more. She smiled a little against his mouth. If he didn't want to be hurried, it wouldn't happen.

Trace's lips moved in a faint smile in return, his warm moist breath gliding over her tongue and melding with her own. His fingers tightened in her hair and she wasn't sure whose heart pounded faster when he slipped his tongue inside her mouth.

She'd thought about this moment...what it would be like. Back in Houston right after she and Matt had returned. For a few nights she'd lain awake in bed wondering what kind of kisser Trace would be. In the end, she'd decided that while he might be a flirt, he'd be considerate. Trace would want to leave a woman satisfied.

Too soon he withdrew, but before she could object, he trailed his lips to the side of her neck. He nipped at her earlobe as he ran a hand down her back, stopping at the curve of her ass. His soft moan against her sensitized skin flooded her with longing. He found her lips again, the urgency clear, his tongue thrusting against hers. She tasted his desire and passion, and fisted her hands, torn between pushing him away and pulling him to the ground with her.

But it was Trace who ended up gentling the kiss. Then drew back so he could see her eyes. His seemed troubled. "What are we doing?"

Looking at him made it hard to answer. "I don't know," she said, burying her face in his shoulder. He held her against the warmth and strength of his chest, and while part of her wanted nothing more but to be right where she was it also scared her to feel so safe, even for these few fleeting moments. "Maybe we should stop until we do."

"I reckon that's wise," he muttered, sounding as confused and miserable as she was.

Neither of them moved. Then Nikki finally took the initiative. She was smarter than to travel this dangerous road only to satisfy a physical urge. Her options were so few already. If she left Blackfoot Falls, she wanted the decision to be hers. Not made for her because of a weak moment.

As she moved farther back, Trace seemed to have trouble letting go of her hand. She seriously flirted with the thought of just saying screw it. Even if they had sex just this one time. Only they would know. That alone told her she'd been right to stop before impulse replaced good sense. The old Nikki had taken that route and look how much trouble that had landed her.

"You don't need to worry about next time," Trace said, scooping his hat off the ground and studying her face. "This doesn't have to happen again."

"It won't."

His jaw tightened. "I was kind of hoping we'd leave that open."

"Oh." She lifted a hand to block the sun. His lips were still damp, and his eyes dilated and dark. Something fluttered in her belly. "Well, it probably wasn't a good idea."

"Says you." With a wry smile, he set his Stetson on her head. It was too big, but it did the job of keeping the sun off her face. "You need one of these."

"A cowboy hat?"

"Excuse me, but this is a Stetson."

"And the difference would be?"

He shook his head in mock disgust, then scratched the side of his neck. "Were you serious? You think it was a bad idea?"

She breathed in slowly and evenly. "I don't know what I think." She could barely stand the disappointment on his face, mostly because of her own frustration. It would be too easy to give in and worry about regrets later. She pulled her phone out of her pocket and made a show of checking the time. "I need to get going. I thought of something I forgot to do."

He didn't look as if he believed her, but then she hadn't expected him to. "You remember your way back to the main road?"

"Yes, and thanks." She backed toward the truck. "Oh, here." She took off the hat and gave it to him, then rushed to retrace her backward steps so they wouldn't start kissing again. "I know I don't have to tell you this, but I'll say it anyway. The kiss should stay secret along with the lessons."

"Understood," he said, settling the Stetson on his dark hair. He hadn't indicated if he agreed, but that didn't matter. "You drive safely now."

"Like a nun."

He might as well have touched her with the way his throaty chuckle shimmied down her spine. "That's an image I'm having some difficulty with."

She grinned and climbed into the truck. It took all her concentration to reverse without hitting a tree or shrub. When she finally got herself pointed toward the road, she checked the rearview mirror.

Trace hadn't moved. He stood with his arms crossed, his long jean-clad legs spread, his boots planted hip-distance apart, and stared after her. The Stetson hid his expression. She could see the shape of his mouth, though, that very clever sexy mouth of his. And wasn't that a terribly stupid thing to notice because now she was getting all tingly.

The grassy trail he'd made was a bit dicey so she was forced to give up the mirror. Five minutes later she was safely on the road that led to town and the Lone Wolf turnoff. Only then did she realize she'd forgotten to ask if he'd be at the Watering Hole later.

"I'M SURPRISED HE'S not here since he didn't show last night." Sadie transferred the pitcher of beer from the tap to the space Nikki had left on her tray.

For a long-drawn-out moment, she debated whether to respond.

Naturally she knew her boss meant Trace because she'd seen Nikki eye the door every time it opened.

"I assume you're talking about Trace?" Nikki's dry smile matched Sadie's. "He was helping Matt at the Lone Wolf for a few hours yesterday. Maybe he's still playing catch-up at the Sundance, or playing with the guests."

Sadie snorted a laugh. "I like the way you say it as if you don't give a hoot. You practice long and hard with that line?"

Nikki nearly told her to shut up, though it wasn't a term she cared to repeat since she'd literally had her mouth washed out with soap when she was seven. Despite her mother's long work hours, she'd been strict enough to keep Nikki in line most of the time. Instead, she picked up the tray, noticed that the blonde with the serious bling sitting nearby seemed to perk up at overhearing Trace's name. Nikki was tempted to ask her if she'd seen him at the Sundance tonight. But what purpose would that serve? If he was MIA, Nikki would only assume he was out with the guest who'd chased after him three nights ago.

Nikki really wished she hadn't remembered that. He'd kissed her. She'd kissed him back. Not that it mattered. They'd agreed not to do it again. Sort of.

"Who needed a fresh mug?" she asked the group of men waiting for their turns to play pool.

Josh smiled and shook his head. She'd liked him even before she found out he was Trace's friend. He was a hand from the Sundance and the kind of guy she could count on if a customer ever got too rowdy. It hadn't happened while she'd been waitressing here, but she'd had to fend guys off twice back in Houston. After that she'd thought about carrying a knife, then decided she'd find a new job before going that far.

"Where's your buddy?" she asked, real casual-like as she set down mugs.

"Lucas?"

"The other one."

"She means Trace." Sam took his shot, cursed when he missed, then straightened and grinned at her. "Don't you, sweet cheeks?"

"Was I talking to you?" Nikki seriously reconsidered the whole knife thing…if only to see the look on Sam's face when she pulled it out. "And keep calling me sweet cheeks if you like your beer warm."

Josh laughed. "He worked late vaccinating the last of the calves. I don't know that he has the energy to come to town."

She blinked. It was because of her that he'd fallen behind on his normal duties. "You mean he actually does real work?" she said, since they'd all expect a wisecrack and not the guilt needling her.

"Trace works harder than any man on that ranch," Josh

said, his tone defensive. "Cole, Jesse, everyone works hard."
He shrugged, almost in apology for being sharp. "But they
don't have double duty like Trace. Rachel relies on him to
handle the guest activities." He glanced sideways to check
for eavesdroppers. "The dude ranch business is a lot more
trouble than you'd think."

He would know. Cole had assigned Josh and Lucas, another hand, to help Rachel run the dude ranch side of the
operation. Nikki was well aware how much the men had to
juggle because in February she'd helped Rachel and Jamie
scramble to make lunches or do whatever when the weather
had forced everyone indoors. She'd seen the annoyed looks
on the men's faces when the women opted out of snow activities and hung out in the barn instead. Not Trace, though,
he always had a smile. He ate up the attention.

She set down the last mug. "Y'all okay? Need anything
else before I go?"

Most of the guys shook their heads and made room to let
her pass. Sam leaned over directly in front of her to grab
some chalk and block her escape route. She reared back,
locking gazes with him, silently daring him to push her one
more time.

"See, this is what I don't get," he said, a grin tugging at
his mouth. He was cute sometimes, when he wasn't being
a smug jerk. "Why pine away for Trace when you can have
me? I'd always have enough energy for you, Nikki. Hell, I'd
even switch from beer to Red Bull if I had to."

That made her laugh. "Pine away? I don't even know what
that means."

"Withering on the vine, honey, as my grandma used to say.
Just waiting and hoping and praying your little heart out he'll
come through that door."

"Oh, God." She waved for him to get out of the way. "I'd
bet your grandma sold snake oil."

He swept his long blond hair back from his face, the grin still there. "A team of wild horses on steroids couldn't keep me away if you were mine."

Okay, he wasn't even mildly amusing now. "I'm not anybody's anything. Now move. I mean it."

"Trace thinks otherwise."

She froze, aware that the rest of the men had quieted.

"All right, Sam, that's enough," Josh said. "You shoulda quit while you were still funny."

Sam didn't even blink. He kept smiling at her.

She had the feeling he was going to wink, and then she'd have to smack him. "You're either delusional or drunk, and now you're cut off." She grabbed the bottle out of his hand.

He only laughed, which made her angrier. She wanted to know why he'd said that about Trace, but she couldn't ask. Sam worked at the Circle something-or-other ranch. It wasn't located anywhere near where she and Trace met today, but on the other side of town. So he couldn't have seen them.

Briefly she glanced at Josh. He'd been quick to stop Sam. Did that mean Josh knew Trace had said something? Or was he just being nice helping get Sam off her back?

"You wanna know what I mean, don't you?" Sam moved to give her a clear path. His faint smirk challenged her to stuff her curiosity and go on to other customers. He was about to find out she was too stubborn to lose that dare.

"Settle up with Sadie before you leave," she said, pushing past him.

"Trace warned all of us to keep away," Sam said. "Made it plain you were off-limits. To everyone but Mr. McAllister himself. Those McAllisters…you know those boys get what they want. Especially Trace."

Nikki told herself to ignore him. It was the smart thing to do. She stopped under the dividing arch to the front of the bar, and turned. "What?"

Sam chuckled. He picked up the beer left on the ledge by the other pool player, and took a swig. "It's true."

"Don't listen to him." Josh snorted with disgust. "Trace never told *me* that."

"Hell, why would he?" Sam cast a dismissive glance at him. "You're a kid. She's so far out of your league you'd need one of those bullet trains to catch up."

Josh turned red.

"Are you kidding?" Nikki's abrupt laugh held no amusement. "I'd go out with Josh before I'd cross the room for you." The other guys seemed to think that was funny, and she decided it was a good time to disappear. "And, you jerk, the 'kid' is my age."

"I'm talking experience, honey," Sam called after her. "We both know you've been around the—"

He cut himself short, and she'd almost made it to the jukebox, but stopped and slowly turned to face him. Sam wore the expression of a man who knew he'd gone too far and wasn't sure how to get out of the mess he'd made. But then, there was no way out. The words couldn't be taken back. People sitting at nearby tables either weren't paying attention or were politely ignoring what had been said. The guys hanging around the pool table, though, they'd all heard.

Watching Sam try not to squirm did little to appease her. She wouldn't let him get away with being a prick, but causing a scene wouldn't help. Dammit. She couldn't decide. Keep walking or make him spell out what he meant. He'd backpedal and apologize before he'd say anything else stupid. Nikki wasn't the only one pissed, and he knew it.

"Sam." Josh stepped in, his jaw tight, a vein popping along the side of his neck. "You don't know when to keep that big mouth shut, do you?"

"I'm just teasing." He tried to shoulder past Josh, who

wouldn't budge. "I don't know anything about Nikki. We were baiting each other and it got out of hand."

"Josh?" Just before he'd spoken up, she'd decided it was better to walk away, but now she moved closer, hoping to keep things contained. "Let it go. Sam's right, he doesn't know me," Nikki said, looking him directly in the eyes. "Because if he did, he'd be sweating and tripping over himself to apologize. I am this close—" she drew her thumb and forefinger together, leaving a hair-thin space between them "—to making sure you're not allowed in here as long as I'm waiting tables. How would that work for you?"

"Shit." Sam scrubbed at his flushed face. "I'm sorry. I really am. Not because you'd get me kicked out. It was a dumb-ass thing to say."

She caught Josh's sleeve when he started to jump in, her gaze staying on Sam. "It was disrespectful," she said, "and I won't have it."

Sam pushed a hand through his hair and briefly looked away. All the guys in back were staring at him, the tension so thick she could stick a straw in the air. "You're right. I was a jerk. The thing is, I like you. I really do, and if it makes you happy to know, I feel like hell."

She sighed. "No, Sam, that doesn't make me happy."

"You leaving might," Josh muttered.

Sam gave him a dirty look. To Nikki he said, "I will, if you want. Leave."

"It's over. Do what you want." She moved a shoulder, truly feeling indifferent and turning back toward the bar where Sadie was probably getting antsy for her to check on other customers.

The whole thing would've gone better if Nikki wasn't feeling off balance. Nothing major, but wow, who was that person who'd confronted Sam? Yet another glimpse of her trying out her new skin. The old Nikki would never have been so calm, refrained from cussing or, sadly, considered that she'd been disrespected. Not that she'd have assumed she deserved the poor treatment, but anger and revenge would've been on her mind.

Had to be Matt's influence, and even partly Rachel's. Or maybe Blackfoot Falls in general. Who knew? Not her. She seemed confused about everything lately.

"How are y'all doing?" She smiled at the three young cowboys getting low on beer. Their table was closest to her but luckily they'd missed the pool room drama. They had prime seats near the jukebox and were busy watching sly women lean over to study the song selections.

One guy smiled back. So did the other two...after they dragged their gaze away from the redhead. "I'll take another longneck."

"Tap for me, and a tequila shot this time, please." The second man had a boyish grin that lightened her mood. "I'm Jerry, in case you forgot."

"How could I?" The little white lie seemed worth it when his smile widened. She'd remember him from now on. "You have perfect manners every time you come in."

His slightly older friend with the narrow face and shaggy brown hair elbowed him. "Guess I'll be switching to soda water. It's my turn to drive." He sighed, then quickly added, "I'm Chip."

"Way to go being responsible, Chip." She held up a hand for a high five. It took a second for him to get it. He wasn't much younger than her but he was so cute the way his eyes lit up as if he'd won the lottery. He started out with gusto, drawing back his hand, then seemed to remember she wasn't one of the guys, and very gently touched his palm to hers.

He had calluses like Trace.

The thought ambushed her. God, she could not let every little thing make her think of Trace. Today had been nice, but it hadn't changed anything between them. And this dreamy thinking crap was why she couldn't allow that to happen. "You know what, your soda's on me."

"You don't have to do that, ma'am."

"It's Nikki."

The three of them grinned, and Jerry said, "We know who you are."

"I'm still learning names," she admitted. "But I'll get there. Y'all need quarters?" She slid a pointed look at the jukebox, where the redhead had been joined by a short dimpled brunette who was eyeing Chip.

He glanced at the woman, then quickly brought his gaze back to Nikki. "You think so?"

"I do." She wanted to laugh at his bewildered expression. Of course she didn't dare. "Here," she said, reaching into her pocket and pulling out change. She only had three quarters, and laid them on the table. "Until I get back."

He passed her a ten. "Will that be enough?"

"Um, I doubt you'll need that many quarters," she said, and left him grinning.

The Watering Hole really was a nice place to work. She liked these customers, and she liked Sadie. Even Sam was okay, or at least manageable. If he hadn't apologized or looked as if he wanted the floor to swallow him whole, she might've felt differently.

She stopped at another table, glancing around to make sure everyone had drinks, then headed for Sadie. Nikki's breath caught. Trace sat on a stool at the end of the bar with a beer in front of him. Part of the bottle was already gone so she knew he hadn't just walked in. What she didn't know was what he'd heard.

7

TRACE'S PATIENCE HAD gotten pretty thin by the time he spotted Nikki out of the corner of his eye. She stopped at Jerry's table and was joking with him and his friends, and Trace had to remind himself this was where she worked and socializing with the customers was her job. It wasn't that he was jealous. Never been the type. But he was beat, and he'd had no business driving all the way to town just to see her.

Hell, they'd been together not more than eight hours ago, and they planned to meet day after tomorrow. He could've waited until then, and stayed home tonight, gotten some sleep. Obviously he couldn't, and that was the problem. It was the damn kiss that had messed everything up. He should've known better.

Nah, knowing what was right and acting accordingly were two different things. That's where he went wrong, he thought, letting his gaze drift toward her. She was wearing her hair down, the way he liked it best.

"I heard you were out at the Lone Wolf yesterday." Sadie wiped the rings off the bar, then leaned a hip against it.

"Yeah, I was helping Matt with a mustang." Trace picked up his beer and took a halfhearted sip. "The place looks good. I hadn't been out there in years."

"How's Wallace doing?"

The concern in her eyes didn't surprise him. Whether she liked the man or not, she'd known him forever. He slid a look toward Nikki.

"Ah, you know her," Sadie said. "She won't talk about him. I quit asking."

Trace smiled. Yeah, he knew. "Matt doesn't think he'll last the week."

"Tell you the truth, I'm shocked he's held on this long. Must be that stubborn streak in him. How's Matt holding up?"

"Seems okay."

"Tore him up bad when Catherine died. I didn't expect he'd get too sad over the old man going, but you never know until the time comes."

Trace studied Sadie for a moment. She was strong, independent, and as far as he knew, never repeated anything that didn't need repeating. He'd always liked her. "I'm thinking that about Nikki. What's your take?"

"Not to say she's cold or unfeeling, but my guess is she'll just be glad when it's over."

He nodded, though he'd been hoping she might've opened up to Sadie a little. Sure didn't sound like it.

"You want coffee instead of that?" Sadie glanced at the bottle he'd barely touched, except to pick it up and put it down.

"I look tired?"

"Half-dead."

Trace chuckled. "That about sums it up. I'll pass on the coffee, though."

"You know you can come in and see her without ordering anything."

He frowned, thought about a denial...

"Don't give me that scowl. I'm old, not stupid." Sadie snorted. "She's coming. Look sharp."

"You're not old. And I always look sharp."

"That grin of yours should be illegal," she said, slowly shaking her head, then wandering toward the other end of the bar.

Unable to help himself, he tipped back in his seat, pretending to stretch, and angled for a better view of Nikki.

She sure didn't look happy to see him. She almost stopped in her tracks. What was that about? The kiss? He thought they'd figured that out.

"What are you doing here?" The brief frown she sent him held an accusation he didn't get. "Josh said you worked late."

"I did."

"So? Should you be drinking beer and then driving?" She leaned over the bar searching for something or other.

It nearly killed him keeping his eyes from going straight to her nice round behind. His mind flashed back to earlier. His hand had rested right there at the curve when he'd kissed her. The temptation to fill his palms had damn near crippled him.

"How long have you been here?"

"What?" he asked, having trouble switching gears. "Ah, ten, maybe fifteen minutes."

"Why aren't you playing pool? Have you been back there yet?" She was acting peculiar, kind of nervous, glancing toward Sadie, then finally slipping behind the bar and setting up shot glasses.

"I don't feel like playing tonight. Who's back there?" He didn't really care. He wanted her to finally look at him, or at least figure out why she wouldn't.

"The regulars."

He watched her make busywork out of pouring two tequila shots and filling three mugs. "You mad at me?"

"No." She looked at him then and sighed. "Why would I be mad?"

"I can't think of a reason. Nothing we hadn't already ironed out, anyway," he said, lowering his voice as if anyone who heard would know what he meant.

She smiled down at the lime she was cutting up, and he was pretty sure she was remembering the kiss. Good. It didn't seem fair for him to be doing all the thinking on it. Lord knew he'd done plenty of that the whole time he'd helped five guests saddle up for their trail ride with Lucas, and then finished vaccinating the rest of the calves. A couple of the women commented on his exceptionally pleasant mood. Probably had something to do with the sappy grin Josh had been quick to point out.

Trace turned to look toward the pool room. Feeling this tired, he wouldn't play if someone paid him. He couldn't take a humiliating loss from Sam, or in front of him. The guy was getting on Trace's nerves. Maybe he'd stick to sitting at the bar. He'd see more of Nikki... The downside was the guests. Harder for the women to get to him around the crowded pool table.

"What?" Nikki asked. "Why are you staring back there?"

"No reason." So that's what finally got her full attention? She was studying his face close enough to see which spots he'd missed with the razor. "Is Josh playing?"

"He was, but I don't know about now. Want me to check?"

"You're jumpy."

"Am I?" She moved a shoulder. "I don't think so." After loading her tray, she came back around to his side. "I have to deliver these drinks. Be right back."

"Okay."

She'd taken a few steps, then backed up. "Don't go anywhere."

"I won't move a muscle." A whole lot more than his muscles were twitching. This was new, her acting as if she cared whether he stayed or left.

Watching her go from table to table did a better job of getting him revved than caffeine. A second wind was coming on worthy of a high gust warning, and if she wanted him to wait until she got off work, he'd be ready for anything.

"Hi, Trace."

He recognized Karina's voice behind him, too close behind, and he did everything in his power not to cringe as he turned his head. "Evening."

"I didn't know you were coming to town or I would've bummed a ride." She slid onto the stool beside him. Her heavy floral perfume almost knocked him off his seat. "Will you let me buy you a drink this time?"

"Thanks, but I'm done." He patted his belly…out of habit… and could've done without the lingering gaze. "Not one of my better ideas," he said with a smile. "Coming to town. I'm too tired to be out this late." He faked a yawn, covered it and murmured an apology.

"Maybe I should drive you home."

His almost-choke was genuine enough. "I have my truck."

Karina smiled. "I assumed you did. Is it a manual? I can handle a stick shift."

"You stay here and enjoy yourself. I'm good to drive." He watched Nikki set down drinks and shoot glances back. "Or else she would've cut me off," he said, with a nudge of his chin.

Karina didn't bother looking. "Is Nikki your girlfriend?"

He laughed, thought what the hell and leaned a little closer. "I'm working on it."

The woman didn't seem the least put off. She nodded, widened her smile. "Does she know?"

"Kind of hard to judge." He was busy tracking Nikki, but Karina's soft laugh brought him back.

"I pity you."

"Why?" He frowned. "She say something?"

"No. Nothing like that." She tilted her head slightly to

the side, studying him as if he was a lab rat. "You're a good-looking charismatic guy and all these pushy city women must drive you crazy."

He drew back, shaking his head and avoiding her gaze. Grabbing the bottle he'd pushed aside, he took a sip of luke-warm beer. "Hey, I'm just a simple cowboy."

"Maybe you were before your sister started the dude ranch, but I doubt it."

"You think differently, you'll be disappointed."

"Would you like to prove it?"

No ignoring the urge to look at her face. She sounded weird, not flirty, sort of like she was conducting business. Her eyes were brown, he noticed for the first time, though not warm and pretty like Nikki's. Karina's eyes were too shrewd. "Are you sitting at a table or would you like me to get Sadie's attention for you?" he asked.

"I just got here." The woman still hadn't broken eye contact. She kept staring at him, and smiling, as if that would make it less rude. "But I can wait for a drink. Let me ask you something…think it would help if you made Nikki jealous?"

"No," he said abruptly. "No, ma'am, I do not." That was it. He'd have to leave. Man, he'd been hoping to talk Nikki into taking a five-minute break and going outside with him. He dug in his pocket for money. "I need to get home."

"I'm sorry. It seems I've given you the wrong impression." Karina laughed and touched his arm. "Though I do have a proposition for you."

Nikki walked up at that exact moment. Even if she'd pretended not to hear, it would've been impossible to believe. No worries there. She didn't bother playacting. Later if he mentioned the annoyed hair flip over her shoulder, or the firm set of her lips that was half pout, half screw-you, she'd deny she ever did those things.

No, she wasn't happy. But she slid behind the bar and plastered on a smile for Karina. "Has Sadie taken your order?"

The blonde shook her head. "I'd love an appletini." She glanced at Trace. "I'm still offering to buy you a beer."

"Pass. Thanks." He tried in vain to catch Nikki's eye. "I'm cashing out."

"You know how much, just leave it." She focused on lining up liquor bottles and finding a suitable glass.

"I'll see you day after tomorrow, right? Same time?"

Her head came up. She frowned. "Oh, right." Their eyes met for a split second, then she swept a gaze over Karina that ended on the drink fixings. "Drive carefully," Nikki murmured.

Unfortunately, at the exact moment Karina said, "I still want to talk to you, Trace."

Nikki kept her eyes downcast and her expression completely blank.

"Good night, ladies." He pushed in his stool. If Karina thought him rude for not answering, so be it. The woman knew she was causing trouble for him. So what that she was a Sundance guest? That didn't excuse her. Partly his fault for opening his big mouth, but enough was enough.

He wasn't going to get Nikki's attention again, and he sure wasn't up to listening to Karina. Halfway to the door, Eli Roscoe from the Circle K stopped him to ask if he'd heard about the next mustang roundup. Since Trace was straddling the fence on the issue, and still doing some reading on the timing viability, he wasn't keen on entering into a hot discussion.

In fact, he wanted to get the hell out of there. Unless Karina had moved to a table and he could have a minute alone with Nikki. He took a chance and looked in that direction. Nikki was leaning toward Karina, intently listening to the woman. Blinking, she drew back, her lips parted in surprise. She glanced at him and burst out laughing.

NIKKI STARED AT HER reflection in the mirror as she brushed her teeth and checked for puffiness around her eyes. Last night she'd managed to get to sleep by two and woke up by nine this morning on her own. Not bad. She was really trying hard to adopt a better schedule. Partly to be a team player, though mostly in self-defense. When these country people said rise and shine, they meant before sunrise. Never gonna happen for her, but she could learn to compromise.

Today she was going to see Trace at their secret spot. It had been her first thought when she woke up feeling like a kid on Halloween morning. Her classmates had all loved Christmas best. Not her. She liked dressing up as someone else. With the right costume, no one could tell she was one of the poor kids. If you weren't riding a shiny new bike by Christmas afternoon, everyone knew you belonged in *that* neighborhood… As if everyone west of Dairy Ashford had the damn plague.

She'd had it easier than most because the boys thought she was hot. Even the private school guys had sniffed around her at the mall, tried to buy her things, asked her to go on dates. The Galleria Mall was where she'd first met Garret Livingston when he was seventeen and she was an easily impressed fifteen-year-old.

Oh, God, she didn't want to think about him now. Or the stupid prom. The dress, no, she refused to think about the dress. That's what always got to her the worst. If she could've changed anything about that day…anything at all…

But that was impossible and she sure knew that by now. She just wished the memories would stop sneaking in. Though they came less often now, and only when she was feeling down. She'd never been able to completely let go of the shame of being needy and foolish and horrible to her mom. So why today? Was her subconscious trying to tell her something? Like she had no business missing Trace. They'd kissed, big deal, and now she couldn't stand not seeing him for one crummy day? It wasn't as if they suddenly had a thing.

Or maybe the problem went deeper. Would getting involved with Trace be repeating the mistake she'd made with Garrett? No, they were two different guys. Sure there was some common ground, like looks, good family, the right name, but lumping Trace in with Garrett was just plain ridiculous. And insulting to Trace. Anyway, her subconscious could just chill. She had no intention of hooking up with anyone in the near future.

She left her room, closing the door behind her. As always, it was quiet in the hall. Deathly quiet. She glanced at Wallace's closed door and shivered. Quickly she shifted her thoughts to the other night and hurried toward the stairs. Thinking about what Karina had to ask Trace had Nikki biting her lip. She'd given her word she'd keep mum, in exchange for the woman's promise Nikki could be there when the bomb was dropped. It sure wouldn't be easy.

With a grin, she swung off the last step and nearly knocked Lucy over. The frail housekeeper lost her grip on the laundry basket she was carrying and it fell to the floor. Amazingly the orderly stacks of folded clothes stayed intact. Lucy bent to retrieve the basket but Nikki grabbed it first.

"I'm so sorry. I wasn't paying attention." Nikki balanced the basket against her hip and touched Lucy's bony arm. As short as Nikki was, she felt tall next to the woman. "Are you okay?"

"I'm fine." Lucy smiled. "I'm not used to having kids around the house again. It's nice."

"I'm twenty-five."

"You and Matt are still kids to me. I just made a fresh pot of coffee. I assume you're headed for the kitchen." Lucy tried to take the basket but Nikki wouldn't have it.

The guilt for not chipping in more was finally getting to her. "Where do you want me to take this?"

Hesitating, Lucy studied her. "Wallace's room."

Nikki's mind started spinning excuses to back out. She didn't want to see Wallace. Even if he was sound asleep and didn't know she was there. It would depress her. Probably make her feel even guiltier for not helping Matt more. "Fine." She'd hand over the basket at the door. "Lead and I'll follow."

Lucy nodded, then held on to the railing as she slowly climbed the stairs. She had to be over seventy, and according to Matt, had known the Gundersons forever. There were no secrets hidden from her. She'd seen Wallace at his worst, breaking family heirlooms in drunken rages and verbally abusing Matt and his mother. But Lucy had stayed loyal long after Matt's mom died, cleaning up after Wallace, making sure he had home-cooked meals and never gossiping behind his back. Matt didn't understand it. He thought the woman was a saint.

Nikki had a different take. To her, the women in Wallace's life, including her own mother, had been spineless fools. Not Barbara McAllister…she'd had the good sense to stay away from Wallace. And still she'd been dragged through the mud that awful February day when the bastard had gotten toasted and called her a whore in front of her sons.

The same day it had finally struck Nikki that she'd been unfair to Matt. Yes, she'd suffered from abandonment issues, but she'd been too self-centered to see that Matt's childhood had been worse. He'd had to live under Wallace's thumb. Four months later she clearly hadn't made much headway. And that wouldn't change at this particular moment. But for her brother's sake she was trying.

She stopped outside Wallace's door and handed the basket over to Lucy. "I'll let you take it from here."

The woman's lined face remained expressionless, though her eyes slowly filled with disappointment. "You should see him. Just for a couple minutes. He doesn't talk much, only stares at the wall when he isn't asleep."

"Another time."

"Wait."

Nikki had already turned away. She didn't want to have this conversation, and she sure didn't want to feel crappy for sticking to her principles. Seeing Wallace wouldn't help Matt. "Look, I know you mean well. And I appreciate all you do for us." She sighed, searching for the right words. "Wallace has never been a father to me. I don't feel anything for him, and I sure don't owe him."

"You're right," Lucy said. "The man's lived here his whole life, yet you don't see folks lining up outside the door for a visit. He's got a foul temper even when he's not drinking. Truth be told, Wallace is getting exactly what he deserves. It's you and Matthew I worry about. Regret can follow a person around like a dark cloud."

"So I've been told." She left out "too many times." "That won't be an issue for me. I promise."

"You claim you don't feel anything for him, but you do." A sad smile touched the woman's thin lips. "You hate him. I see it in your eyes, and I can't say that I blame you. Trouble is, hate can fog a person's thinking."

Nikki silently watched her reach for the doorknob. "Can I ask you something?" she said before Lucy opened the door.

"I'm listening."

"Why stick around? After Catherine died, it was only Wallace. And you continued to clean up after him, cook, bring groceries. I don't get it."

"No reason you should." Her gaze narrowed and her mouth tightened. "My family has owed the Gundersons for a long spell. And that's all I'll say on the subject." Then she went through the door to Wallace's room, closing it behind her.

Much as Nikki was relieved to be off the hook, now she was curious. Matt would've told her if he knew anything about Lucy's family owing the Gundersons. He'd chalked up her loyalty to his mother's talent for convincing people to make difficult promises.

Cinnamon-laced Columbian brew scented the air from the foyer into the kitchen. Lucy always added a heaping spoonful of the spice to the dry grounds, and Nikki was totally hooked. A plate of poppy seed muffins sat near the coffeepot. Homemade, naturally, and after sampling one last week, she was a fan. It was way too early to eat, but she grabbed one anyway, and carried it with her mug of coffee to the front windows.

She was hoping to spot Matt working outside. She hadn't expected to see him in Wallace's office, looking grim and sitting at the massive old desk. Ledgers and stacks of paper sat on the rawhide couch to his right. Since the door was open she didn't hesitate to poke her head inside.

"Hey."

Matt lifted his gaze. "You're up early."

"I'm a country girl now."

"Right." Despite his smile, he looked tired. "I'm glad you're here. I wanted to talk to you."

Something was wrong. She thought of her room with longing, then braced herself and entered the office. "What's up?"

"First, no need to panic. This isn't a request, strictly information." He slowly exhaled. "Wallace is refusing liquids. If you wanna say goodbye, now might be the time."

"Thanks for letting me know," she said calmly, tamping down the sudden denial swelling inside her and making her chest ache. She managed to keep her expression blank. "Anything else?"

Matt shook his head. His eyes searched her face, probably looking for a sign she was human, before lowering to her hand.

She'd squeezed the muffin into a misshapen lump.

8

NIKKI KNEW BETTER. Nothing good came of waking up before noon. She should've stayed in bed. But it was too late for that, now that she was already at the Sundance.

"Hey." She found Rachel and Hilda making lunch in the big modern kitchen with its stainless-steel appliances and gleaming pearl-gray granite countertops. "I came by to see if you needed help today."

"Oh." Rachel seemed surprised, which she would since Nikki never dropped by without being asked or calling first. "That's nice of you. But I think we're okay. Most of the guests are out kayaking."

"With Trace?" God, Nikki hoped she didn't sound as desperate and panicked as she did to herself. They were still supposed to meet since she hadn't heard otherwise. And she wanted to see him. Needed to see him. She didn't know why. She just did.

"No, he had them yesterday. It was Josh's turn. Grab something to drink and sit down."

"Have you eaten yet?" Hilda asked, studying Nikki from head to toe. The housekeeper's round face darkened. "You've lost weight, *chica.*"

Odd remark considering Nikki wore tight jeans and an old

tank top that had shrunk from too many washings. In fact, had she been thinking, she would've changed before leaving the house.

"I've eaten," she lied, and slapped the side of her thigh. "This baby fat hasn't gone anywhere, I'm afraid."

Rachel opened the fridge to return a jar of mayo, but stopped to give her the stink eye. "Don't think I won't hurt you because you're Matt's sister."

Nikki managed a smile. "Have you talked to him today?"

"Early this morning. Why?"

"He say anything about Wallace?"

"It's sort of a given." Rachel's eyes narrowed. "He normally ends up part of the conversation. Tell me what's going on."

Taking a deep breath, Nikki pulled a chair out from the table and sat down. "Matt said if I want to say goodbye, I should do it today." She glanced at Hilda, who was making the sign of the cross. The woman had been with the McAllisters forever. She knew Wallace was worthless, but she still acted human. Why couldn't Nikki find that kind of compassion?

Rachel sat at the table with her. "So, did you?"

"See Wallace?" Nikki frowned. "No. I came here to cover for you in case you want to be with Matt."

Rachel's expression held no censure, simply concern and kindness. "Maybe you should be with him."

Nikki sighed and stared out the window over the sink. All she could see was the sky, so clear and blue. "I think I might make things worse."

"Come on, you can't really think that." Rachel reached over and rubbed her arm. "Your brother loves you, and he understands."

"I don't want to disappoint him, but I can't fake that I care. Because I don't. I—I—" Nikki looked at Hilda. "I saw you say a brief prayer and I thought, why can't I be that charitable? What's wrong with me?"

"Oh, Nikki." Rachel scooted her chair closer. "You barely know the man, and he's been nothing but horrible to you, to your mom, everyone."

"What I hate most is how he treated Matt. I can't forgive him for that."

Rachel shrugged. "Neither can I."

"But then I'm not hurting Wallace. It's Matt who's suffered because I've been selfish, and now it's too late." Nikki rarely cried, but she was starting to choke. Kindness did that to her.

"This is my honest opinion," Rachel said, her gaze steady. "Both of you were better off with you keeping your distance. Two extra hands might've helped, but not the tension. Knowing how you feel, Matt never wanted you waiting on Wallace or taking care of him. He'd rather you make a clean start here, create good memories."

In a way this was making Nikki feel worse. Rachel was warm, supportive and perfect for Matt. And Nikki adored her. So how could she feel jealous at the same time? She struggled daily with her petty thoughts. Her relationship with her brother was still new but already changing since he'd hooked up with Rachel. They were great, both trying to keep her from feeling like the odd person out. Nikki's contribution was to disappear as much as possible.

"I have a confession." Hilda put a glass of orange juice in front of Nikki. It was understood she'd better drink it, or else. "Yes, you saw me making the sign of the cross. You know why? Because I know Mr. Gunderson is not going up there," she said solemnly, pointing at the ceiling.

With a straight face, Rachel asked, "You mean upstairs?"

Nikki was able to hold back a grin. Until Hilda glared at Rachel, who started laughing and turning as red as a tomato.

"I wouldn't even expect that from your brothers." Hilda turned to the stove, no amusement in her face.

"I'm sorry," Rachel said. "I shouldn't have joked. I'm tired though that's no excuse." She stood. "If you don't need me I'll go see Matt."

Nikki didn't dare look at her again. If she did, she'd start laughing and not stop. It was one of those weird inappropriate reactions you couldn't explain. And she'd hate to upset Hilda. She reminded Nikki of her grandmother, and she'd been just as kind, throwing in Spanish words here and there, trying to make Nikki feel at home. She didn't have the heart to admit her Spanish vocabulary consisted mostly of cusswords.

"I can help," Nikki said, once Rachel was gone. "I'll wash sheets, towels, do whatever you need." She picked up the glass and gulped down some juice before Hilda turned to her.

With amusement dancing in her dark eyes, Hilda waved a wooden spoon in the direction Rachel had disappeared. "Lucky for that one she doesn't get into more trouble." Hilda looked at Nikki. "How about a bean and cheese burrito *chica?*"

Nikki blinked. Her go-to comfort food. Of course Hilda would know…she was from a poor Texas border town and had grown up much like Nikki. "I would love one," she said.

"Red hot sauce?"

Nikki nodded, saw Hilda shake her head again at Rachel and started to laugh. The short break she'd taken to compose herself meant nothing. She couldn't stop laughing.

Until her eyes filled with tears.

TRACE HAD SEEN Nikki's truck so he knew she was at the Sundance. He figured she'd be in the kitchen with Rachel. He entered the house through the mudroom and found her sitting at the table.

Her head was bowed, her long dark hair loose and hiding

her face. Her shoulders shook, and it kind of sounded as if she was laughing. But he prepared himself to be wrong. Pulling off his work gloves, he lifted a brow at Hilda. She shrugged, then gestured for him to stay back. Bad sign.

He liked being around women, no secret there, but one who was crying made him want to pack a tent and stock a cooler. But then Nikki wasn't just any woman, and he had offered her a shoulder to cry on.

"Hey." He moved closer. "Nikki?"

She looked up with wide watery eyes. "What are you doing here?"

He smiled and pulled out a chair.

"I know you live here. I just thought you'd be out in a pasture somewhere." She wiped her cheek and sat straighter.

Damn, but he still couldn't tell if she'd been crying-crying or laughing-crying. Either way he wanted to pull her into his lap and put his arms around her. He didn't care that Hilda was watching, but Nikki might. "You okay?"

"Yeah, fine." She shoved her hair back, wincing when her fingers pushed through a tangle. "You missed Rachel by a few minutes."

"She lives here, too. I'll see her." He leaned over and used his thumb to wipe a dark smudge from her cheek.

She jerked away. "What are you doing?"

He held up the evidence on the pad of his thumb. Makeup, probably, and he didn't know why that made him think those were real tears but that's what he concluded.

"Better not be here to cancel on me," he said, and her gaze darted to Hilda. But he'd been careful how he worded it so no harm.

"No." She dabbed under her eyes. "I know Jamie's away for a few days so I stopped by to see if I could cover for Rachel so she can go see Matt."

He wiped his hand on his jeans, not sure what to do. With Hilda there it was hard to talk. "Is that where she went?"

Nikki frowned. "Oh, Rachel. Yes, but she may not have left yet."

Trace shrugged. "I was just wondering…"

"Did you have lunch?" Hilda asked.

"An hour ago. In the bunkhouse with the boys."

"So now you like Chester's cooking better than mine?"

"Come on…" He grinned. "You don't believe that, Hilda. You know you've ruined me for any other woman. Or I should say cook."

Chuckling, she washed and dried her hands. "I'm making bean and cheese burritos if you want one. But first I have to check the clothes in the dryer."

He might've believed her had she gone in the right direction. "What's going on, Nikki?"

"Nothing." Her brows lifted, and her eyes widened just enough to fake surprise, but he wasn't buying it.

Leaning forward, he slid a hand behind her neck and pulled her face toward him. Her stunned expression looked real enough now. "Were you crying?" he asked, and brushed his lips across hers.

"You must've been out in the sun too long," she murmured, but didn't retreat. "You can't do this here in the kitchen."

"If Hilda or Rachel or my mom walked in right now, think they'd be shocked?"

"Yes, I do. *I'm* shocked."

Trace smiled and used the tip of his tongue to dampen her lower lip. "Tell me the truth."

"About?"

"Everything."

Nikki's warm sweet breath slipped out, tempting him to do more exploring. "Dream on," she whispered, her lips lightly moving over his.

He applied more pressure, making it a real kiss, until it started getting out of hand. "I'd settle for the reason you were crying."

She pulled back, sighing. "I wasn't crying, really. I was a little…tense…and Rachel made me laugh, and then I couldn't stop. You know how that is…. Sometimes laughing and crying sort of blur together."

"Is it about Wallace?"

"Jesus, it wasn't about him." She jumped up, and he caught her arm.

"Wait. Don't get all bent. I just wanna make sure you're okay." He held on to her while he got to his feet.

"I'm fine. I'm always fine."

"You don't have to stand on your own all the time, Nikki." He ran his palms down her bare arms. "You're not alone anymore."

She stiffened. "What does that mean?"

"People here care about you."

Her chin came up, and her gaze locked on his face. A hint of challenge glinted in her eyes. "Who?"

Trace hadn't expected the question and it stopped him. "Matt, for one," he said. "Rachel. Hilda. Jamie." Nikki kept staring at him. "Sadie." He touched her cheek, wondering why he was having trouble including himself. It wasn't as if the *L* word would come into play or that she was asking for a commitment. And he did have feelings for Nikki. Her small sad smile got to him. "And me. I care about you."

"You don't have to say that."

"I know I don't." He finger-combed her hair, massaging her scalp and watched her lashes flutter, then droop. "If I hesitated it was only because I figured how I felt was understood."

"That's lame."

He smiled. "I know that, too."

"You're forgiven as long as you keep this up." She let her

chin drop as he worked his fingers toward the back, all the way down to the top of her spine.

Her small-boned frame felt fragile, and even though he was careful not to rub too hard, her whole body rocked under the pressure of his fingers. But he kept kneading out the tension, feeling her relax until her forehead rested against his chest and she let out soft moans.

When he couldn't stand it anymore, he tightened his arms around her and cradled her to his chest.

Slowly she brought her chin up, tilting her head back to look at him. "I thought we were supposed to cool it until we figured out what we're doing."

"I'm not starting anything, just letting you know I'm here."

"So that's what you call this."

"Why?" He dipped down for a quick kiss. "What do you call it?"

"Trouble."

"Ah. You've got me there." He stared down at her lips, fascinated with their silky smooth texture, at how they plumped into a perfect pout. When he met her dazed eyes, his jaw clenched. "You," he whispered, his whole body tensing, "give trouble a new meaning."

She pressed her breasts against him, peeling off another layer of his control. The little imp knew exactly what she was doing. A few more minutes and he wouldn't be interested in any more talking.

Nikki clutched his shoulders and arched her back, just a little, enough to expose more of her slender neck and throat. "You realize Hilda could walk in at any moment."

"Hell, she's probably listening at the door to see if it's safe to come back."

"God no."

She froze when his answer was to kiss the tip of her chin. He traced her lips with his tongue, getting too heated for his own good. But Nikki wasn't responding. Not in a way he'd hoped, anyway. Her body had stiffened and now she was trying to evade his mouth.

He stumbled back a step but held on to her. "What?"

"Hilda."

"I was joking."

"No, you weren't."

"You'd really care if she caught us?"

"Yes." She swung a gaze toward the dividing door to the dining room.

"You keep surprising me."

She shrugged a shoulder as if she wasn't happy with her reaction but there it was. "You'd be embarrassed, too. And don't deny it."

He didn't, even though she was wrong. After being with the family for over thirty years, Hilda was as much a part of the Sundance as any of them. She'd waded through the hormone-driven teen years of her own son, Ben, as well as Trace and his brothers. Not much left that could embarrass him or Hilda.

Tightening his arms around Nikki, he brushed his lips over her ear. "I get you moaning loud enough she'll never come in."

Nikki let out a startled laugh. "You're that sure of yourself?"

He grabbed a handful of hair and tilted her head back again. The curve of a woman's throat had never been a turn-on for him, not like this. He kissed the soft silken skin, knowing damn well he was only torturing himself. This had to end soon. Before it got out of hand. Before he couldn't remember the reason they'd stopped the other day. Matt. Rachel. Nikki's fresh start. She didn't need a complication right off. Or to have folks gossiping about her. They all knew he wasn't the type to take on a relationship. He hadn't been serious about a girl since high school. He just hadn't met anyone who made him want to put on blinders.

She made a muted purring sound that vibrated against his mouth. It might as well have zipped straight to his cock. Not much separated common sense from a wild need to drag her up to his room. He had to calm down.

"And the guests?" she asked, letting her head fall back even more. Eyes closed, lips parted, ready for him to slip his tongue inside. Taste the sweetness he'd already sampled.

"What about them?" He breathed in her dizzying scent, warned himself again to back off. The argument was already fading in his mind.

"One of them could walk in on us."

"So?"

She smiled, swaying enough that he had to tighten his arm around her waist. "This is crazy."

"Maybe we should start your lesson early."

"My—?" She opened her eyes. "Oh, right," she murmured, blinking away the confusion. "What time is it?"

The big round clock hung on the wall to his left. He strained to see it without losing ground, fearing if he let her go, the moment would be lost.

Nikki pushed on his arm, trying to look for herself. He relaxed his hold and she broke away. The sensible side of his brain told him it was for the best. His body strongly disagreed.

He turned to the clock, so worked up inside that he had to squint to focus. No way that much time had gone by since he'd come inside. He cut off a curse at the last second. Cole wanted to meet him in the east barn, and Trace had agreed to be there five minutes ago.

"What's wrong?" Nikki touched his arm, then quickly withdrew.

She shouldn't have to worry about a casual touch, that was the kind of thing he'd been trying to avoid. If he hadn't pushed, she might not have given it a second thought. He lightly squeezed her shoulder, then went to the window and looked outside for Cole. If he were on time, he'd be waiting at the entrance.

"I forgot I was supposed to meet Cole. I'll come look for you when I'm done and we can talk about later." When he saw his brother standing outside the stable talking to Karina, Trace grinned. He knew by the look on Cole's face he'd been caught off guard and would do anything to escape. That gave Trace a couple more minutes with Nikki.

She joined him at the window, and the instant she spotted them she broke out in a huge smile.

"What's that for?"

"Nothing."

"Yeah, sure looks like nothing." It reminded him to ask her about the other night. "You and Karina, at the Watering Hole, what were you laughing about?"

She turned away, shaking her head. "I can't tell you. I promised."

"Well, that's a fine thing." He caught her arm, spun her back to face him. "You trust her more than you do me?"

"You want me to break a promise?"

Hard to argue when she put it that way. "Give me a hint. Did it have anything to do with what I told her about you and me?"

Nikki lost the smile. "What did you say?"

Trace cringed. He should've thought before putting himself on the hot seat. "She asked if you were my girlfriend and I sorta said I was working on it."

"Sorta said?"

"Yeah, okay, I said it, but it was in self-defense…not to mention your fault."

She folded her arms across her chest. "I can't wait to hear this."

"I was getting a group ready for a ride and thinking about us kissing and…well…I might've looked a little sappy when I helped Karina into the saddle and I worried she'd gotten the wrong idea."

"Oh." Nikki's lips again curved into a smile, but a strange one. "What she told me had nothing to do with that."

Well, hell, that didn't tell him squat. "I didn't know you two were so chummy."

"That was the first time we'd really talked." She lifted a shoulder. "I like her." She moved closer, lowering her voice to a teasing whisper. "If you can't keep your mind on work, then no more getting down and dirty."

"We haven't even gotten dusty yet." Trace tried to sneak an arm around her waist but she danced out of reach. "Come on now, I only have a minute before I have to go save Cole."

Nikki suddenly got serious. "What if Karina repeats what you told her and it spreads?"

"About me working on you?" He dismissed it with a shrug. "No one will think anything of it. You're in the clear, and people will figure that's just me being me."

Regret hit him instantly. Even before her expression fell and her body tensed. A lot of people considered him a player, and Nikki didn't have evidence to the contrary. He needed to explain….

Hilda reentered the kitchen.

Too late. He had to let it go for now. At least he still had later when they could talk in private. "I gotta go get Cole," he said, looking directly at Nikki. "I'll see you soon. Same time?"

She hesitated, and he tried to hold her gaze, tried to silently communicate that he needed to see her. But he knew he'd lost her the second her lips lifted in a faint smile. "Another day, okay?"

Dammit. He glanced at Hilda. She'd busied herself with

stirring a pot on the stove, but she could still hear. Saying anything more would only make Nikki uncomfortable. He let out a frustrated sigh and headed for the door. Maybe he had been that guy, but meeting Nikki had changed his ways. He just wished he could convince her of that.

9

"NIKKI?"

She turned at Sadie's voice rising above the boisterous laughter from the back room crowd, and saw her boss motioning that she needed her. Nikki had been idly chatting with Chip and another cowboy while she cleared off a table, so she grabbed the last two dirty glasses and headed to the far end of the bar where Sadie waited for her.

"I can't figure out why it's so slow tonight," Sadie said, glancing around the room.

"It's not that bad."

"Huh. Most of the hands got paid two days ago. Can't tell me they've already gone through their paychecks."

Nikki leaned on the bar, studying Sadie. Her comment was odd enough, but to call Nikki over for that? Maybe the phone call she'd gotten a while ago had something to do with her strange mood. On the first ring Sadie started grumbling like she always did, swearing to disconnect service because it was a waste of money and she was tired of passing on messages from angry wives. But she hadn't yelled for anyone to get home before they had to sleep in the barn.

Maybe she'd heard from her daughter. They didn't speak often, but the one time Mariah had called while Nikki was working, Sadie had gotten depressed after hanging up. Part of her wanted to ask if Sadie needed to talk, but the gesture didn't come naturally. Nikki hated people butting into her life so she tried to stay out of theirs.

And today probably wasn't the time to change her ways.

Turned out everything had sucked, from getting up early to the reminder that Trace was exactly the kind of guy she'd feared. He was a player. Guys like him used to be exciting to her, a challenge she couldn't resist. No more.

Okay, the thrill hadn't disappeared, but she needed to work at tamping down her attraction. She'd been bitten twice already by hooking up with guys who had more charm than substance. That was enough. At least she'd had the sense to cancel her riding lesson. The consolation was so tiny she wanted to scream.

"Um, Sadie, did you want something?" she asked when it seemed as if nothing more would be said. "You know, when you called me over?"

"Oh, right." Sadie waved an acknowledgment when a customer yelled they needed beer in the back. "Why don't you go on home? No need to stick around when it's this slow."

"It's really not that bad. Everyone's drinking steady." Nikki didn't get it. What was going on? They'd been less busy quite a few nights and Sadie had never suggested she go home. "Did I do something wrong?"

"No." Sadie reached over and squeezed her hand. "You've been a godsend. Don't go thinking that way. I just don't see the point in us both hanging around on a night when it's a one-person job."

"But I don't mind. I—"

"I don't wanna hear any more about it," Sadie said, shaking her head and coming out from behind the bar.

"I can check the back first, see who needs beer."

"Would you just go on?" Sadie could be impatient and

irritable with customers, but she'd never used that annoyed tone with Nikki.

"I have five open tabs sitting beside the register. I can close them out before I leave if you—"

"We're getting thirsty back here," one of the pool players yelled loud enough to be heard at Abe's Variety down the street.

Sadie craned her neck to see who it was, then hollered, "Keep your pants on, Leo." She turned back to Nikki. "I've been doing this a long time, honey, I'll figure it out. And don't worry, I'll make sure to set aside your tips."

"I'm not worried about that." Feeling like a kid who'd just been suspended from school, Nikki watched her amble toward the back. Except she hadn't done anything bad. If there had been a complaint about her...

A sudden thought struck as Nikki crouched to grab her keys from the shelf under the cash register. Maybe Sadie needed the money. The tips weren't great tonight, but working alone could amount to a nice chunk of change. If that was the case, Nikki was glad to leave the business to Sadie. She dug into her pocket for the tips she'd collected earlier. It was only twenty bucks or so, but it could help. She made sure Sadie wasn't in view, then stuffed the bills into the older woman's tip jar sitting on the rear counter.

On the way out, customers ragged on her about leaving, asking if she had a hot date. She sent wisecracks back at them, but she couldn't deny feeling at loose ends. If it was about money, she would've worked for free, she didn't care. The Watering Hole was as much home to her as the Lone Wolf.

She stopped on the sidewalk and sucked in a deep breath. Directly in front of her, Trace's truck was parked at the curb. He was leaning back against the door with his arms folded and the brim of his hat pulled down low. As if he were waiting for someone. For her?

"Hey," he said, pushing off the truck.

"What are you doing?" She hadn't seen him inside. Unless he'd slipped in and out while she and Sadie were talking. "Were you in the Watering Hole?"

"Nope. Just got here. Come sit in the truck with me for a minute."

"What is this?" She wished she could see his eyes better. "How did you know I'd be out here?"

"Come here and I'll explain."

"No." She squeezed the set of keys until it dug into her palm, then pulled her arm back when he reached for her. "I'm staying right here until you tell me what's going on."

Main Street almost always quieted down after six-thirty. At nine, with the Food Mart and Abe's Variety closed, the town was dead. Two trucks and a blue sedan were parked in front of the diner. Other than a pair of headlights coming toward them from the south, nothing moved on the street.

She wouldn't even have noticed the headlights except Trace seemed weirdly interested. He stood silently watching the vehicle's approach, his mouth a grim line as the car passed.

"Dammit, Trace, you're scaring me."

"I don't mean to." He caught her this time, tightening his grip on her wrist when she tried to shake him off. "Would you settle down?"

"No, I won't. First Sadie sends me home like I'm a kid who's disobeyed, then I come out here and—" She gasped at the feel of her breasts being crushed against his chest. His rough treatment stunned her.

"I'm sorry if I pulled too hard." He put his free arm around her before he released her wrist. Apparently he wasn't contrite enough to let her go.

"What is wrong with you?" With the light from the bar's sign shining in his face, she could see his eyes now. They were dark and serious, and she knew something bad had happened. "Is it Matt?" Her heart nearly exploded from merely voicing the question. "Tell me he's okay, Trace. You tell me right now."

"Matt is fine." His genuine look of surprise reassured her more than the words. "It's Wallace."

"He's dead?"

Trace nodded. "He passed away about forty minutes ago."

"Why did you scare me like that?" She punched his shoulder. "Damn you." Pausing, she struggled to take a breath, and shivered in the warm summer air. It was finally over... the waiting and having to watch her brother care for the man who'd shown him nothing but contempt. She should feel relief. Still she felt nothing. "I thought it was Matt. God."

"Now will you get in my truck?"

"Why? I drove—" She stared at him as things started falling into place. "Is that why Sadie told me to go home? She knew about Wallace?"

"I called her after Rachel phoned me. She and Matt, we all thought it was best that I come get you before you heard the news from someone else. Doc Heaton gets summoned this late it means either he'll be delivering a baby or certifying a death."

"Was that him in the blue car?"

"Yep. Somehow his comings and goings seem to spread fast around here."

Nikki sighed. She couldn't be mad at everyone for caring, no matter how misguided. When Trace hooked a finger under her chin and gently tipped her head back, she said, "If you're looking for tears there aren't any."

A faint smile curved his mouth. "I want you to be okay, that's all."

She twisted away from him, lifted her hands, palms up. "Look, I'm fine. Just like always." She twirled all the way around. "See?"

"Yes, good." He gestured to his truck. "We should go."

Screw his patronizing tone. She sidestepped him and headed for her own truck. No, not hers, the pickup belonged to the Lone Wolf. She didn't have anything of value. Never had, probably never would. The hell with the Gunderson trust fund. Matt considered half the ranch hers, she didn't.

"Nikki…what are you doing?"

"Going home like a good girl. Isn't that what everyone wants?"

She kept walking without glancing back, wanting to run. But that would only convince Trace she was upset and needed a babysitter. The stupid door was locked so she readied her key. Everyone in Blackfoot Falls left their vehicles open, windows half-down, everyone but her. She hadn't broken the habit yet, and damn she wished she had because her hand shook too hard to get her key inserted. Of course she'd chosen the only truck at the Lone Wolf that didn't have a remote.

Sneaking a peek to locate Trace, she saw him standing right where she'd left him. She didn't have to see his watchful eyes to know they tracked her every move. On the third try she got the door open and climbed in, quickly checking the rearview mirror to see him slip behind the wheel of his own truck. She knew he'd follow her, but there was nothing she could do about it.

Cursing her unsteady hand, she missed the ignition twice before pushing the key home. After she'd pulled away from the curb she realized she hadn't checked for oncoming traffic. So what? No traffic except for her and Trace. If she passed a single car in the next fifteen minutes to the Lone Wolf she'd be surprised.

Her hands were freezing, and she rolled down a window instead of using the heat. The warm air rushed in. She glanced at the speedometer, saw how fast she was driving and eased her foot off the accelerator. She hadn't even left the town limits yet. All she needed was to get stopped and ticketed. Though she was pretty sure Roy was on duty, and the deputy would probably let her skate with only a warning.

Forcing herself to breathe in deeply shouldn't have been hard. But she couldn't seem to draw in enough air and panicked for a moment. Trace was the problem. He followed close behind and, God, she didn't want him seeing her fall apart.

No, no, that wasn't it. She didn't even understand where the thought had come from. Even after what Matt had told her this morning, she hadn't truly believed Wallace would die soon. She figured the bastard was too stubborn and mean… he'd hang on just to make everyone else miserable. Her worry wasn't that she'd fall apart, but that she wasn't prepared. Her emotional bank was empty, void, not even a hint of compassion had surfaced. How was she supposed to react appropriately?

She knew Rachel was with Matt, and Lucy had to be there, too. Maybe Petey was at the house. The wrangler knew the family well. And the doctor, of course, he'd still be there when she got home. Or maybe not…if she slowed down. What if she waited a couple of hours? She'd call so Matt wouldn't worry….

No, she'd feel like shit if she ditched him. As if that wasn't exactly what she'd been doing for weeks. He'd given her a chance to help even things out by asking her to see Wallace a final time. Oh, Matt had claimed he meant only to give her the facts this morning, but she'd understood the subtle suggestion that she step up and say goodbye, and she'd walked out anyway. She'd been too stubborn and defiant to give so much as an inch, and now… Oh, God, she didn't know.

All she wanted was to stop thinking.

It was too quiet. Listening to music would help. She turned on the radio, knowing the signal sucked this far north. Her CDs were tucked in between the passenger seat and the console. She fumbled trying to find one, momentarily lost control of the wheel and weaved into the other lane.

She checked the rearview mirror, half expecting Trace to overtake her and force her to pull over. But he continued to stay at a sensible distance behind, and somehow the knowledge that he hadn't overreacted calmed her. Deciding against risking her neck over a CD, she clutched the steering wheel with both hands and stared at the dark highway ahead. And the stars. Lots of them twinkled in the clear inky sky. So different from Houston with its pricey high-rise condos and gleaming skyscrapers blazing with lights. Not exactly a star-friendly place.

So Wallace was dead.

Okay, Nikki had known his end was coming, but she hadn't seriously considered what life would look and feel like after he was gone. Matt planned on easing out of the rodeo circuit and running the Lone Wolf. He insisted half the ranch was hers, but she didn't give a crap about inheritance. The place belonged to Matt, period. She had no interest, no investment in the Lone Wolf, emotional or otherwise. She was only here in Montana because...

Her breathing stalled again, and she forced herself to pay attention to what her body was telling her. She was in major stress mode.

With Wallace alive, she'd been coasting. Any decision regarding her future she'd easily shelved for later. Matt had been busy with his care, and she'd scrambled to make herself unavailable. A tiny part of her had hoped by the time Wallace was gone she'd have grown attached to the ranch and Blackfoot Falls. She liked her job and most of the people she'd met, but enough to make this her home? She couldn't say. So where did that leave her? Aside from feeling utterly confused.

Startled, she saw the turnoff to the Lone Wolf up ahead. Of all the nights for the drive to seem short... She slowed to make the turn and, yep, Trace was still right behind her. Maybe it was best he'd be there with her. He'd be a distraction and Matt wouldn't fuss over her so much in front of Trace.

She forced herself to concentrate on the narrow private road, looking out for deer that liked to come bounding out of nowhere and dash in front of the truck this time of night. Her hands were cold again, actually freezing and stiff, and she let go of the wheel to shake the circulation back into her fingers.

She hadn't made it far when the lights became visible. Normally she wouldn't see the Lone Wolf for another half a mile. But tonight, God, so many lights were ablaze they lit the sky. Had someone flipped every single switch on the property? How many people were there? And why? Had they come to see her father in his last hour?

The thought stopped her, the truth hitting her so hard it was impossible to breathe.

Wallace was…or had been…her father. It didn't matter how much she hated him. Or that they'd never bonded, and she'd resented him as far back as she could remember. Her father, the man who'd given her life, had died tonight. And she had the horrible, horrible suspicion that she had wanted something from him after all.

Just once she'd wanted him to look at her, really see her as his daughter. Give her that special smile fathers reserved for their little girls. Let her believe that in his heart he was happy she existed.

God, how could she have been such a fool?

In spite of herself, in spite of all the nasty things of which she'd known he was capable, she'd secretly been hoping Wallace would tell her he regretted abandoning her and her mother. People changed. She had, so why not give him the benefit of the doubt? But she'd never gone to see him at the end, so how could he have told her?

In her heart she knew he hadn't changed, and he hadn't

cared about anyone, not even Matt. To think she'd pitied her brother for yearning for Wallace's approval. She was no better. And the really sad thing was, she'd prided herself in being too smart to buy into such emotional nonsense.

Her foot slammed on the brakes before she knew what she was doing. Not much room for her to pull over, but she managed to park halfway off the road in case anyone had to squeeze by. She cut the engine and jumped out, knowing Trace would've stopped, as well.

She couldn't go inside. Or be anywhere near the house. Funny, how only minutes ago she'd worried people expected tears she couldn't shed. Now she feared the flood gates wouldn't hold.

"Hey, honey, you okay?" Trace had gotten out of his truck and was walking toward her. The night was black except for the pickup's headlights, and she focused on his long legs closing the distance between them.

She flung herself at him, knowing he'd catch her, confident he wouldn't let her fall no matter what.

His arms came up around her, and she burrowed against him, burying her face in his chest, hugging him around the waist, holding on as tight as she could.

"Nikki," he whispered when she shuddered. "It's okay, honey, I've got you."

What was it about Trace that made her want to trust him? She couldn't figure it out, and right now she didn't care. "Take me someplace," she said, finding comfort in the sure steady beat of his heart against her cheek. "Anywhere we can be alone."

He stroked her back. "Matt's expecting you."

"It's fine. I'll call him."

"I know it'll be hard to—"

She cut him off by gripping the back of his neck and pulling him into a kiss. He resisted at first, and then she didn't have to stretch so high because he lowered his head and kissed her back. His breath was warm, laced with mint and coffee. She parted her lips for him, offering only panic and desperation in return.

He touched his tongue to hers, teasing and tempting her to join the dance. She clung to his neck, tugging him closer, willing him to kiss her harder and deeper and help her forget what she had to do.

Instead, Trace gently peeled her hand from the back of his neck. "Nikki," he whispered. "This isn't the time."

"Make love to me, Trace. Please. Take me away from here. Anywhere." She heard his sharp intake of breath and pressed her advantage by moving his hand over her breast.

"Sex isn't the answer."

She yanked her blouse from her jeans, then started unfastening buttons. He caught her hand on the third one. "I know you want me," she said, jerking his shirt hem loose. She slid her palm underneath the fabric, over his flat belly, up to his bare chest, knowing she was turning him on. "Deny it if you want, but I'll know it's a lie."

"I'd never deny it."

"So? Come on. You must know someplace private around here. Your truck has a backseat, let's go park somewhere."

"Ah, Nikki." He moved his hand away from her breast to touch her face. She sucked his forefinger into her mouth and rubbed her body against his. What he said didn't matter, he was hard, really hard. "I know you're hurting," he said huskily. "But do you really want to worry Matt? Or Rachel and Lucy?"

She almost bit him. She hadn't asked anyone to care about her. Wrong thing to do. If anyone got too close they'd see how cowardly and selfish she really was, and what then? Would they still think she was worth their concern?

Pulling up his T-shirt, she pressed her mouth against his

warm skin. He smelled strong and masculine, and she had no doubt he could make her forget a whole lot. With the tip of her tongue she tempted his resolve and sampled the slight saltiness of his skin. His breath came out harsh and raspy, and she knew he was on the verge of giving in to her.

"Come on, Trace," she murmured against his chest. "Last chance." She cupped his erection through the thick denim fly, pressing against his cock with her palm, using just enough pressure to make him moan.

He jerked. Stilled. Then pushed her hand aside. "Nikki, stop. I mean it."

She froze, not sure what to do next. She could've sworn she had him. "Goddamn you, Trace," she said, and shoved him back. "Damn you."

"Wait." He tried to capture her hand, but she dodged him and ran for her truck.

She was too angry, hurt and embarrassed to hear anything more. He probably assumed she'd make a beeline for the highway. Good. Let him waste time blocking the road. Exhaustion had dug in to every pore and was slowly leveling her. She wanted to crawl into bed, pull the quilt over her head and sleep for three days. Maybe she'd find that today had only been part of a bad dream.

Her name carried on the breeze, and she muffled his voice by starting the noisy engine. By the time she pulled into her normal parking spot near the house, she saw Trace's headlights right behind her. Taking the flagstone walk, she counted four extra cars, two of them unfamiliar. Trace met her at the front door.

"You didn't have to follow me," she said. "I'm a big girl."

He smiled. "I came to pay my respects to Matt."

Nikki swallowed, briefly closed her eyes and breathed in

deeply. She put her hand on the doorknob and told herself she could do this. But she only believed it when Trace touched the small of her back.

10

"THIS IS WAY TOO MUCH food." Nikki eyed the huge bowl of cubed potatoes, then frowned at the whole ones she had yet to cut up. "Everyone's going to be eating potato salad for a month."

"Don't bet on it." Rachel used the back of her wrist to dab at her tears. "Any time you want to trade is okay with me. We don't need as many onions."

"No, thanks." Nikki started to smile, then sighed.

She probably should show more gratitude. Here Rachel, Hilda and Mrs. McAllister were doing all this work to feed people after Wallace's funeral tomorrow. Plus they were dirtying their own kitchen. All because Lucy insisted on a proper church service and burial.

Matt hadn't argued with her, though Nikki doubted he cared one way or the other. She'd stayed completely neutral. What mattered most to her was that this whole thing be over and done with. Let everyone get back to normal. Including her. Last night Sadie had refused to let her work again. It had really pissed Nikki off. She'd already done her dutiful best the night Wallace died.

So what she'd remained in the corner praying for a shot of tequila until Wallace's body was taken away and everyone left. At least she'd been present, and that was more than anyone should've expected. Rachel hadn't batted an eye, and that was one of the things Nikki liked about Matt's girlfriend. She was totally nonjudgmental and supportive at the same time. Must be a McAllister trait. Trace was the same way.

Nikki hadn't seen him since that night…. Actually, it had been after midnight when he left. She'd gone up to her room five minutes later, feeling no less embarrassed than she had when he'd turned down her offer.

God, the humiliation still hadn't disappeared. If things had gone differently and they'd had sex? Hard to even imagine how she'd be feeling. He'd been right to refuse. She kind of owed him, though she was happy to ignore the incident.

"Will there be booze served at this thing?" she asked.

"Huh. I don't recall it coming up." Rachel turned away from the cutting board, making a face and sniffling. "I am so over dicing onions. This has to be enough."

"No." Hilda kept stirring the refried beans on the stove, but frowned at the small mound in front of Rachel. "We need at least three more."

"Seriously?"

Hilda gave her a look that said she was quite serious.

"I'll do it," Nikki said. "This is for my fa—" She almost choked on the word. Where had *that* come from? "For Matt and me," she muttered, focusing her attention on laying down the knife. "Let's trade."

"No, it's okay." Rachel gave an exaggerated sniff. "Really."

Hilda shook her head and went back to humming while she stirred.

Nikki sighed. The onion-dicing job would be better for her. Every now and then, she got a little teary-eyed. She couldn't explain it, other than a general feeling of sadness. But if the waterworks started, at least she could blame the onions.

"I want to do it, honest." She tried to elbow Rachel aside.

"No, go call Matt. Ask him if we should offer beer and/or liquor tomorrow."

"You know him," Nikki said. "He won't care."

"Yeah, maybe we should ask Lucy."

"She's not home," Mrs. McAllister said, carrying in bags of beef and vegetables she'd gone to get from the freezer. "She's delivering the clothes Wallace is to be buried in."

Nikki stared down at the potatoes. His death hadn't completely sunk in yet. His bedroom door remained closed. Every time she went upstairs it was a jolt to realize he wasn't there.

"Thank you for doing all of this," she said quietly. "I can't say I understand…I know how horrible he was to your family."

"Wallace wasn't always difficult." Mrs. McAllister dropped the packages on the counter and patted her arm. "As a young man he could be quite charming. Besides, this really isn't for him."

Charming.

The word alone was like an intolerable high-pitched scream to her ears. Nikki's mother had used the same description. He'd charmed his way right into her bed and made promises he never intended to keep. But then Wallace had made a daughter, too, and hadn't kept her, either.

Dammit, she'd also made a promise, one she had yet to honor. Why was she finding it so hard to call her mom? Why did her mother even care that he was gone?

She smiled at Mrs. McAllister, who'd moved to the sink. "We're trying to decide whether to serve booze tomorrow. I can pick some up after I leave here."

"That's your call. Some people do, some don't." She narrowed her eyes at something outside the window. "What in the world is that woman thinking? That stallion was still rearing not ten minutes ago. Trace doesn't need to be distracted."

Nikki and Rachel hurried to the window. He was in the

corral with a horse, holding a lead, trying to calm the animal down. A blonde Nikki recognized from the bar had slipped between the railings. Dividing his attention between her and the now bucking stallion, Trace waved frantically for the woman to get out.

Rachel cursed under her breath. "I'll go get her."

It was too late.

Trace lost the lead, fell hard and rolled clear of the horse's hooves by a scary few inches. The blonde scrambled to safety outside the corral. A cowboy ran from the barn to help Trace regain control of the stallion.

"It seems we need to have another talk with the guests after dinner." Mrs. McAllister's hand was at her throat, her face pale.

"I'm going to have one with Eve right now," Rachel said, steam practically coming out of her ears.

"No, don't. Trace is going to talk to her."

Watching him walk over to the guest, Nikki knew he was hurt. He subtly probed his left shoulder and winced. After speaking with the woman for a minute, he gave her the usual killer smile. But as soon as he started walking toward the house putting her behind him, the smile abruptly vanished as if a switch had been flipped.

"My poor brother," Rachel said. "I've been overloading him with guest stuff and with all his other duties he's exhausted." She sighed. "These women have been driving him nuts lately. He's so sick of them. I'll have to figure something out."

"Other than his shoulder he seems okay," his mother murmured. "He reminds me of your father more and more each day. Same mannerisms, same temperament. Of all your brothers he's most— Oops, he's headed for the mudroom. I doubt he'll appreciate us standing around watching him. I have to run upstairs, anyway."

As soon as she left, Nikki looked at Rachel. "Trace is like your dad?"

Rachel blinked. "Yeah, I guess he is."

Quite a compliment considering what she'd heard about Gavin McAllister. "Does he know that?"

Rachel shrugged. "Beats me." Her gaze returned to the window. "I hadn't really thought about it before."

Nikki saw that he was close to the house. "I need to talk to him."

"Go," Rachel said, with a nod at the mudroom door.

"Thanks." It would be private in there, at least for a few minutes. Trouble was, she didn't know what she wanted to say except to apologize for the other night.

He entered from outside just as she came in from the kitchen. His brows lifted in surprise. "Hey, I didn't know you were here."

"Are you all right?" She stopped when he did, standing a few feet away and feeling awkward, unnerved that her first instinct had been to touch him.

"Fine. Why?"

"I saw you fall."

Disgust transformed his expression. Flushing, he squeezed his eyes shut and muttered a mild curse.

"Don't be embarrassed. It wasn't your fault."

He yanked his gloves off and squinted at her. "Who said I'm embarrassed?"

"Okay," she said, trying not to smile. "Forget I said that." She cleared her throat. "And while we're at it, can we forget about the other night?"

"Why?" He shrugged, doing a better job than her of controlling a smile. "What happened?"

She fixed her gaze on his shoulder because she was still worried about him, but also to avoid his eyes. "Thank you for not taking advantage of my stupidity."

"Told you. It's forgotten." He reached for her hand and drew her closer. "How are you holding up?"

"Numb, confused, overwhelmed…" She sighed. "Anxious to get back to work. Sadie wouldn't let me go back last night."

"She was right not to," he said, rubbing her arm.

"I'm better off keeping busy."

"Yeah, but you never know what bonehead thing a customer will say that could set you off. I'm not naming names, mind you."

Nikki smiled. "What else hurts besides your shoulder?"

"Ah, Jesus." He let her go and plowed his hand through his hair. "Nothing. Nothing hurts."

"Well, I see your ego is in working order."

One side of his mouth lifted and he caught her chin. "Lucky for you I hear people in the kitchen," he whispered.

"Yes, they're waiting to fawn all over you."

"Well, hell." He lowered his hand and yanked a glove back on. "Thanks for the warning."

"Wait." She laughed. "Where are you going?"

"Where there aren't females trying to either get me hurt or patch me up." He stopped with his hand on the doorknob. "How long you gonna be around?"

"Until we're done preparing food for tomorrow." She shook her head. "We're making a ton of stuff. Way too much. I keep telling everyone— Go, before it's too late."

Trace smiled. "I'll see you later, huh?"

Nikki nodded, amazed how much better she felt just talking to him. "You'll be there tomorrow, right? At the funeral."

"Of course I will." He gave her a long gentle look that stirred a whole new batch of strange emotions inside her. "Standing right beside you."

TRACE HADN'T PULLED close enough to the curb to be legal. But that was just too damn bad. Main Street wasn't exactly bustling at suppertime and he didn't plan on staying long anyway. He opened the heavy oak door to the Watering Hole and backed up onto the sidewalk when Nikki stormed toward him.

"Oh." Frowning, she stopped, leaving enough room for him to close the door. "What are you doing here this early?"

"What am *I* doing here? Just this afternoon we talked about you not coming back to work too soon."

"Actually, no, we didn't." Shoving her fingers through her hair, she dislodged her ponytail and ripped off the elastic band. "You agree with Sadie. I don't."

"So, are you working or not?"

"Sheila's in there," she said. "Sadie asked her to cover for me tonight." Nikki growled and groaned at the same time, her restless gaze sweeping the street. "I'm so pissed I can't see straight. Why does everyone think they can make decisions for me?" She exhaled a harsh breath, then eyed him with a frown. "I assume you came for a beer. I'll have one with you."

"I didn't come here to drink. I came to talk some sense into you."

Her lips parted and she just stared at him for a long drawn-out moment. "Seriously?"

"Yeah, seriously." He tugged on a lock of her hair. So soft and shiny, he wanted to grab a whole handful. "You gonna stand out here and argue with me?"

She sighed, her shoulders sagging as if the fight had suddenly left her. "I haven't called my mom yet."

He took her arm and guided her the few feet to his truck. "Are you saying this is cosmic justice? I doubt you're being punished for procrastinating."

"What?" She looked at him and laughed, then sighed again. "Oh, Trace, I want life to be normal. I need normal."

"You might want to look up the definition." He opened the passenger door, feeling that familiar tug in his chest when she looked up at him with those wide trusting eyes. "You waiting for me to lift you up?"

"I'm kinda normal. You just aren't used to city women."

"Right." He snorted a laugh. "Because I haven't had my fill in the past year."

"Hey, what about me? Had enough of me?"

"Sometimes I can't decide if I wanna kiss you or strangle you." He had her trapped between the door and the seat, his body blocking her escape. "Does that answer your question?" He leaned close enough to kiss her, close enough to see the gold flecks of excitement dancing in her warm brown eyes.

"I get that," she said with a small grin. "Where are we going?"

"For a ride…maybe find a place to park on one of the ridges."

Her brows lifted.

He smiled, draping one arm over the door and letting his weight bring him even closer to her. "And watch the stars."

Nikki laughed and pushed him back so she had room to climb up by herself. But she caught the sore spot on his shoulder, and he winced before he could stop himself.

She got in and turned in time to see it. "Oh, no. I'm sorry. God, Trace, are you bruised? Let me see."

"It's fine. I'm fine. Everything's fine," he muttered, made sure she was clear, shut the door and rounded the hood.

"Why don't I drive us in my truck?" she asked, eyeing his shoulder as he slid in behind the wheel.

"No, thanks. I saw how you drive."

"Hey." She drew her knees up and hugged them to her chest. "That was different."

"You want to call your mom now?"

She shot him a startled look. "Yeah, I guess."

"Want me with you when you call?"

After taking a deep breath, she nodded, which shocked

him. He hadn't expected her to let him listen. If she changed her mind before they found someplace private, he'd understand.

He pulled a U-turn and drove toward the Sundance. She stretched out her legs, dug into her pocket and brought out her cell phone. All she did was stare at it, though, then turn her head to watch the scenery.

It was still light. Usually he liked the longer June days, but not this evening. He would've preferred a nice dusky glow. The upside was they'd probably be able to catch a decent sunset.

"You're not taking me home, are you?" she asked ten minutes into the ride. "Because I won't—"

"Nope."

She twisted around to check the mile marker they were passing. "I don't want to go to the Sundance, either."

"Good."

Settling back, she stared at her phone again. "Wherever we're going, will I have cell service?"

"Yep."

"Can you manage more than one syllable while you drive? Because if not I can take over."

Grinning at her, he lifted his boot off the accelerator, then slowly made the turn.

Sitting taller, she peered out the windshield. "Oh. I know where we are. I think."

Trace didn't correct her. She'd see soon enough she hadn't been up to this particular meadow. He shifted to four-wheel drive and took them up as far as the eroded trail would allow. The last of the yellow and purple wildflowers dotted the mountainside. Another week and they'd fade.

"Wow, this isn't where I thought we were. It's pretty, but why are there flowers up here and nowhere else?"

"It's cooler because of the elevation so they hang on longer. A month ago there were three times as many. Wait until next spring. You'll see all kinds of wildflowers in back of the Lone Wolf." He cut the engine and suddenly her attention went straight to her phone.

"Okay, I'm ready to do this."

"Want me to take a walk?"

"No." She grabbed his arm, surprising both of them. "I don't understand why she wants to know," Nikki said, letting him go to press speed dial. "I mean, she hasn't even seen Wallace in over twenty years. What difference does it make that he's dead?" She held the phone to her ear with an unsteady hand. "She's finally getting married to a decent man and moving to— Mom? It's me."

Nikki turned away from him, her back stiff and tense. He lifted the center console out of the way and angled his body, sliding closer to her so he could reach her shoulders.

She jumped, but when he started to massage and work out the knots, she relaxed. "How are you? Getting packed?" She paused. "No, everything is fine." Another pause. "How did you know?" she asked, her voice softer. "Yes, he died in his own bed. Last night. No, actually the night before but I've been kinda busy helping make food for after the funeral. Fine. I promise."

Letting her chin fall forward, she quietly listened to whatever her mother had to say as he continued to carefully work his fingers into the layer of muscle above her shoulder blades.

"No," she said after a minute. "I'm with a friend. No. No. Why does it matter?" Nikki sighed, and Trace smiled, wondering if she realized she sounded like an annoyed teen being interrogated. "Rachel's brother, okay?" She stiffened again. "Yes, it's Trace."

So she'd spoken of him to her mother. Well, wasn't that something? He splayed his hand and ran it down her back, giving her the bonus rubdown. She gave a tiny shiver and sent a glare over her shoulder.

He winked at her.

Rolling her eyes, she faced the passenger door again but made it obvious by leaning back that he was to return to his slave duty. "You sound good. I expected you to be upset." Nikki got quiet, listening for a while and really starting to relax.

"Oh, Mom, I'm sorry. Though I should've known, because I couldn't figure out why you'd want the details." She laughed. "If you knew how much I was dreading this call—" Nikki went perfectly still. "What? Say that again."

All the tension he'd managed to work out returned full force. She leaned forward as if she wanted him to stop touching her. So he lowered his hands, feeling as though he'd caught some of her anxiety.

"What did you tell him?" She chewed her thumbnail, something he hadn't seen her do before. "No, no, I understand. How was he? No, I meant…could you tell if he'd been using?"

Her voice had lowered but of course he was still able to hear everything, and she had to know.

"Good for him." She started to rock, a slow small motion that might be giving her comfort but made him edgy as hell.

It was crazy how much this woman continued to get to him. How many nights had he lain awake trying to figure out what it was about her that had him feeling as if he was running a race without a finish line. He'd tried taking small time-outs since she'd come back. Staying away from the bar, away from her, hoping to get his head straight.

He'd even tried convincing himself to call the pretty blonde he'd met at the Billings auction. She'd given him the green light and two phone numbers. Might've been smart to take her out to dinner, see what happened. Right now, he couldn't even remember her damn name. Hanging around Nikki did that sort of thing to him. Made no sense. Until he'd met her, he even preferred blondes. What was that about?

Clenching his jaw, he noticed the way her shoulders had slumped. She was still rocking, and he wanted to grab the phone from her and stop whatever was making her unhappy. The riding in on a white horse crap wasn't his style, either. He liked things nice and easy. More than once he'd been accused of hiding behind his "trademark smile." Not that he gave a damn. Why mess with something that worked just fine?

"No, Mom, really...I swear you did exactly right. I've got to go, though. Say hi to Edward for me, and I'll talk to you before you leave for Mexico City." She disconnected the call and with a sigh, dropped the phone onto the seat beside her.

"You okay?"

She scooted back, found his arms and pulled them around her as she leaned against his chest. "The clouds are pretty with those streaks of pinkish-orange."

Closing his eyes, he inhaled the floral scent of her hair. His arms rested loosely just below her breasts. She only wanted comfort, and he wanted to give her that but, damn, she wasn't making it easy.

"Trace?"

"Hmm?"

"Thanks for being a friend," she said softly.

He smiled, feeling more than a little deflated, and kissed her hair. Okay, so maybe he'd grown bored of nice and easy. Besides being gutsy, loyal, independent and sweetly vulnerable, Nikki was by far the most complicated woman he'd ever met.

11

NIKKI CROSSED THE THRESHOLD into the small stone church and froze. God help her, why were there so many people? Most of the pews were filled. Up front was the dark cherry casket Matt had chosen. She'd gone with him to be supportive and agreed on the style while barely sparing a glance. Vases of flowers had been set on either side and in front of a podium.

Lucy, Matt and Rachel had driven together and were already seated in the first pew. Nikki took a deep breath and pulled her shoulders back, ready to make her way down the aisle when she saw the portrait of Wallace. Taken when he was a much younger man, the blown-up head shot sat on an easel to the right of the casket.

That was it for her. She couldn't seem to make her feet move. Vaguely she recalled Matt and Lucy discussing which picture to use, but Nikki hadn't seen it. Not this one, anyway. Her mom had once had a similar photo. She'd kept it in a silver frame she polished every day, sitting on a nightstand in the shabby bedroom she'd shared with Nikki. Right after Nikki started kindergarten the photo had disappeared. Just like the man himself had vanished two years prior.

"Nikki?" Trace touched the small of her back. She looked up at him and he smiled. "Let's find our seats."

She nodded, took the arm he offered, and then leaned on him the whole way to the front pew. Matt stood, kissed her cheek and indicated the seat next to him. She saw the rest of the McAllisters and Hilda sitting directly behind and gave them a shaky smile before sinking down to the hard wooden bench. A moment of panic nearly set her off, but she relaxed when Trace sat on the other side of her and squeezed her hand.

The minister took his place behind the podium and started with a prayer. Nikki had no idea what he was saying. Her goal was to avoid looking at the picture of Wallace. It stirred up too many bad memories. Of course the stupid easel stood only a few feet away. She couldn't even look straight ahead without being aware of Wallace's image. But each time she felt her chest tighten, she squeezed Trace's hand and he squeezed right back. That's all it took to calm her, which in itself should've terrified her.

That, and how since Wallace's death she'd been thinking of him as her father. Before it had been easier to think of him as Matt's father and not hers, or the dying man down the hall. Mostly she realized she'd been better off without Wallace in her life. Matt had been the unlucky one. But somehow she had to get through the service, so she decided to focus her thoughts on Trace…thoughtful, dependable, handsome Trace with his killer smile and big heart. Had she ever encountered someone so unexpected? She didn't think so. She turned her head a little to look at his profile, and met his watchful green eyes. This time he rubbed his palm against hers, creating a pleasant warm friction. Much better than the squeeze.

God, she wanted to feel his arms around her like yesterday when they'd sat quietly watching the clouds turn pink and orange. He'd known exactly what she needed.

The sudden awkward silence might as well have been a gunshot in the dark. Lost in her own thoughts, she had no idea what was going on, or where they were in the service.

Okay, now she was nervous again. She glanced at Trace and saw that he was looking past her and Matt. She turned her head and watched Lucy walk stiffly to the podium. Her hands were as white as the handkerchief she was wringing.

Trace lowered his head and spoke close to Nikki's ear. "No one volunteered to give the eulogy."

Oh. Poor Lucy.

The woman was so small you could see only her face over the podium. Nikki imagined that was fine with Lucy, who noisily cleared her throat, started to speak, then cleared her throat again. After about a minute she mumbled something about knowing Wallace his whole life, then gave in to tears. Matt got up and returned her to the pew.

Nikki bit at her thumbnail, a habit she'd kicked long ago. She didn't want her brother to feel as if he had to say something. It wouldn't be fair. Everyone would know he was lying if he said anything nice. How awful would that be…?

Rachel seemed worried, too, twisting in her seat to look at her family. Probably giving Cole or Jesse the eye.

Trace released her hand and slowly got to his feet. She hadn't noticed the black jeans or that he was wearing a long-sleeved black shirt and his new boots. None of it mattered. But she wasn't thinking very clearly.

He looked nervous standing behind the podium trying to loosen his collar and keeping his gaze high. "You folks out there who went to school with me know how much I *love* being up here," he said, and people laughed. Eyes downcast, he took a deep breath. "Most everyone knows there was bad blood between Wallace and my family, and I'm not going to stand up here and pretend otherwise. We had our differences." He shrugged. "But I'm truly sorry Wallace has passed on. He was too young to die and it's a shame he didn't have more time to get to know the man his son had become or the fine daughter he brought into this world."

Nikki held her breath. Trace was looking at her, and she suspected so was everyone else. She would've died herself right on the spot if not for the affection on Trace's face. Somehow she managed to give him a shaky smile.

"Wallace could be mean when he was drinking, though I heard it from people who knew him back in the day that he wasn't always so ornery. No matter what, the one thing nobody can take away from him is that he produced two exceptional children who will do the Lone Wolf proud and who make our community a better place." He tugged at his collar again. "I guess that's all I got to say."

On his way back to his seat, Matt shook his hand. Then Nikki grabbed it. She didn't say anything since she didn't trust her voice, but the rest of the service seemed to go fast. Half the people showed up at the cemetery. She only went because she felt she had to, though she would've preferred going to the Lone Wolf with Hilda, Rachel and Mrs. McAllister to handle the food.

Trace stuck by her side, then followed her back to the house. She headed straight for the bar that she'd personally stocked yesterday and poured them each a drink. Screw anyone who didn't like it. They were welcome to help themselves.

"What is this?" Trace asked, squinting at the glass.

"Tequila." She held hers up to the light. "I hope."

"Now, that doesn't sound good." He smiled. "You okay?"

"I am now. I can finally breathe again." She took a sip. "You don't drink hard liquor, do you? I can get you a beer."

"This is all right."

Nikki hadn't even gone to the kitchen yet. But she saw the casseroles, roasted chicken and salads already spread out on the dining room table and figured she'd get cleanup duty. Several people she didn't know came up and introduced themselves. Others officially welcomed her to town and extended a blanket invitation to Sunday suppers. Trace was included as if they were a couple. She hoped that hadn't upset him, though if it had, he didn't let on.

She smiled and nodded a lot, even when she didn't understand some of the older people, and just hoped her responses were appropriate.

"Hey, McAllister." A guy walked toward them holding a plate heaped with food and grinning. He was about Trace's age but thick around the middle. "I thought you were gonna shit a brick up there talking in front of everybody."

"I tell you what, Buck. I did just like Mrs. Wilson told us in the ninth grade. Pretend everyone in the audience is naked. If I looked queasy it's because I got to your ugly ass."

Buck laughed. "Hi, Nikki. I met you once at the Watering Hole. You probably don't remember. But I am sorry about your pa."

"Thank you," she murmured, wishing she was better at faking a smile. As soon as Buck left to find a chair, she told Trace, "We're too close to the food. That's why so many people are stopping. Let's move."

He didn't seem to mind the suggestion and hustled them into the empty living room. "There are a lot of folks here. I doubt we'll be alone for long." He brushed the hair off her face. "You look good. I'm glad you're holding up."

"Thanks to you," she said, and he shook his head. "Yes, you. What you did…back at the church…" She swallowed. "Thank you. For all of it. Even though it's not quite over," she said, glancing out the window at the cars coming down the driveway. "I feel as though a big weight has been lifted."

"I'm glad." The tenderness in his smile reached his eyes. "You seem relaxed." Something behind her drew his attention. "There's Sadie. When is she letting you back to work?"

"Oh." Nikki groaned, turning to glare. Not that Sadie noticed. "I'm so mad at her. She's making me wait until day after tomorrow and she won't budge."

"Good."

"Gee, thanks."

"Tomorrow night. You and me, we're going to Kalispell for dinner." Trace snuck in a quick kiss. "And I'm not budging, either."

"Wow, ALL THIS TRAFFIC is making me nervous." Nikki turned to catch the movie listing being flashed on a monitor outside a theater. She didn't recognize the titles, but then she hadn't kept track of new releases since moving to Blackfoot Falls.

Trace was shooting looks at her with one raised eyebrow. "Yeah, okay, so this isn't Houston but a year from now let's see how itchy you get to come get your ya-yas out."

"Ooh, so touchy." She sat back, checking out restaurant signs and the people crowding the sidewalks. "I was kidding. This is fun. Looks like a lot of tourists, though, what's that about?"

"We're close to Glacier National Park, which brings in the summer tourists. In the winter they come to ski Big Mountain. Whitefish Mountain Resort isn't far from here. Neither is Blacktail Mountain Ski Area. I know you didn't get to see enough snow in February. We'll go up there once the resorts open and you'll have your fill."

That was a few months off. Would she even still be in Montana? "Do you ski?"

"No," he said, a hint of regret in his voice. "I thought I'd learn but life seemed to get in the way. Why? You wanna try?"

"Oh, no. Not me. Watching from indoors with a cup of hot chocolate is more my speed." They stopped for a red light, giving Nikki the chance to read a banner strung to a corner post. "They sure have a lot of festivals here. I wouldn't mind coming to one. Have you been?" She watched a couple hurrying to cross the street against the light, then turned to Trace when he hadn't answered.

He was staring at her, a faint smile on his handsome face. His dark hair was as long as she'd seen it, curling at his collar and occasionally falling across his forehead. She was glad he hadn't cut it.

Reaching for her hand, he intertwined their fingers, his callused palm feeling warm and right against hers. His hunter-green Western shirt was brand-new, probably just out of the packaging. She knew for sure because he hadn't ironed out the creases from where it had been folded. The thought made her smile.

Trace brought her hand to his lips and kissed it, lingering to inhale the vanilla-scented body cream she'd rubbed everywhere.

"Have I told you how beautiful you look?"

"Once when you picked me up and twice at dinner." She tried to ignore the heat surging to her cheeks. It had been quite an eye-opener to discover she was more comfortable with Trace teasing and flirting than she was when he got serious and looked dangerously sexy. "But don't let that stop you."

His mouth curved in that same slow patient smile he'd given her across their candlelit table an hour ago. She'd had a glass of wine, something she did only on special occasions. His concession was to drink his beer from a wineglass. That had made her laugh, which she suspected had been the point.

Of all the ridiculous things, her nerves were getting the better of her. She couldn't explain it. She was supposed to be more worldly, more sophisticated and…what was the word… *blasé?* Yeah, that was it. Anyone may have assumed tonight was something she'd done a thousand times. Not give a second thought to having a really hot guy come to her door, take off his hat, kiss her and tell her she looked beautiful. Oh, not just say the words but really mean it, so that she'd see the truth in his eyes.

She'd certainly tried to give the impression of a woman

who'd seen it all when she started at the Watering Hole. And it was partly true. Her fast life in Houston was so different from anything here in Montana, people here wouldn't get it. But right now she was out of her element, and she had the feeling he knew it. The shift in power would've bothered her more if it was anyone but Trace.

He released her hand, slid his arm across the back of her seat and leaned in to her. Their lips barely touched when a horn honked behind them. The light had turned green.

Trace cussed under his breath and hit the accelerator.

Nikki laughed. "What are we doing after the driving tour? Not that I'm not enjoying this."

"I'd planned on checking out what movies are playing, but I don't know…" His gaze started at her exposed shoulders then slid down the front of her strappy sundress. "I should be showing you off."

"Oh, God, there you go being sexist again."

"I know, and I don't care."

She shook her head, faking disgust. The thrilling way he'd practically devoured her with that look trumped political correctness. "Then we should go dancing."

"Um…"

"Relax. I'm kidding." She twisted around for a second look at the fancy hotel they'd passed. So much nicer than the motels she'd seen closer to the highway.

Nikki turned back and faced straight ahead. She couldn't tell if Trace had noticed the hotel or her interest in it. Of course sex was on her mind. And she'd bet her savings she'd been thinking about how tonight they had the perfect opportunity. The heated looks were hint enough. But after throwing herself at him the other night, the subject was still touchy for her.

"You seem restless," he said. "Is there somewhere you wanted to stop?"

Suspicious that he *had* seen her check out the hotel and was teasing her, she studied his profile. He wasn't trying to hold back a smile or anything. "No. Just getting the lay of the land as they say." She sighed, wishing the horn hadn't interrupted their almost kiss. "I haven't had many dates."

He frowned, darted her a glance. "What's that?"

She sighed again. The thought had passed through her mind so many times she wasn't sure she'd meant to say it out loud. "I haven't had many dates. Not the real kind. Like tonight with you picking me up at the house."

"Why not?"

"It wasn't like that in high school." She shrugged. "My friends and I did group things and then sometimes paired off. After graduation I worked nights, even when I went to community college, so I didn't have time for a social life."

"We went out in groups, too. Mostly to football games or rodeos, so I get that. But what about proms or dances or just dinner and a movie?"

Nikki bit her lip. Ten years later and she still cringed just hearing the word *prom*.

"Obviously you think I'm an old-fashioned country boy, and you go right ahead—"

"I don't think that at all. Don't put words in my mouth."

"I see you trying not to laugh." He caught her hand again. "A woman accepts an invitation from me and she's gonna get picked up at her house, and seen to her door at the end of the night."

"Oh, boy, if you ever have daughters their teen years won't be pretty."

He let out a short laugh. "Probably not."

"I like that you're all gentlemanly and chivalrous." She saw the corner of his mouth quirk. "I do. It's nice. I wasn't laughing." She braced herself. "I had a bad prom experience," she said, hoping she was right, that telling Trace would ease the tightness in her chest. "I'd met this boy at the mall when I was fifteen. Garrett was seventeen, a private school kid. His family was loaded. Obviously he didn't live in *my* neighborhood.

"Anyway, he followed me and a girlfriend around, asked for my cell number, tried to buy me lunch. I kept saying no and—" She smiled sadly. "And probably giggled a lot. Garrett was hot and funny and smart, and not what I was used to, so of course I was flattered. Every day for a week he showed up at the food court where we hung out. I have to admit, I looked forward to seeing him. Finally I gave him my number and agreed to go to a movie. The next weekend it was a party and then another party after that. It went on for three months.

"My friend was convinced he was using me, but he'd never pushed me into sex. We made out a lot but nothing too hot and heavy. I mean, I think Garrett really did like me. He even asked me to go to his prom." Taking a breather, she studied the familiar storefronts they were passing. Were they headed back to the highway?

Trace squeezed her hand, then released it to use the turn signal. "I'm still listening," he said quietly.

"His friend heard him ask me and I should've gotten a clue from his shocked face. But I was too excited. I'd seen a dress at the mall, a very expensive dress, and I was already planning the argument I'd give my mom. We couldn't afford it, but I begged and pleaded so I wouldn't feel out of place with all the rich girls. She gave in, then two days before the prom, Garrett called it off. He was still going, but he had to take someone else."

She saw that he was pulling the truck over to the curb. "What are you doing? Don't stop." Part of the reason she was able to talk about it was the situation. Trace had to divide his attention, and somehow that made it easier. "Please."

The helpless uncertainty in his eyes touched her. "All right," he said finally, and returned to the flow of traffic.

"Garrett said he felt terrible. His parents had hired a limo for him, and a photographer to take pictures, and he said he was sorry but they wouldn't understand him taking someone like me to the prom. He had college to consider and didn't want to piss them off." She refused to look for Trace's reaction. "He said nothing had to change between us. He wanted to continue seeing me."

"What a bastard." He spat the words with so much anger she had to look at him. The veins stuck out on his neck.

"It's okay. Jeez, it was so long ago. Anyway, I should've known better. My friends tried to tell me."

"Tell you what?" Now he sounded angry with her friends.

"That I should stick to my own kind, and that Garrett was too class conscious and would eventually kick me to the curb." She laid a hand on his thigh. "I don't think about him anymore. Honestly, I don't. Of course it crushed me at the time. I was only fifteen. In my head Garrett was like Wallace and I was mad at myself for being as stupid and weak as my mother."

Trace shot her a confused look.

"Like I said, I was fifteen. One week my mom was the enemy, the next she was my BFF. I took so much crap out on her." Nikki shuddered at the memories. "What still bothers me is the dress. She busted her butt working overtime to buy it for me. And I couldn't return it because—" Oh, God.

She laid her head back against the headrest watching the thinning crowd. No use admitting she'd been the worst possible self-centered idiot. It wouldn't change anything. Already she'd said too much. Trace was probably disgusted with this new glimpse of her. She was pretty sure they were about to reach the highway that would take them back to Blackfoot Falls.

Her hand still rested on his thigh. She could feel the muscle bunch when he applied the brake. "I wanted you to know how special tonight was for me," she said. "That's why I told you all that. I wish I hadn't gone overboard— I don't know, it felt good to let it out. It's the first time I've told anyone."

"I'm glad it was me." He caught her hand when she tried to pull it away and put it back on his thigh. "Garrett's a damn fool but I can't say I'm sorry he blew it with you," he said as they passed the last two motels on the outskirts of town.

If he had planned on a more intimate night, she'd screwed that up. She'd treated him like a friend, not a lover, and she'd never had a man play both roles in her life. And, dammit, Trace made a really great friend. Although she still wanted to find out if she was right about what kind of lover he'd be. She'd sure thought about it often enough.

She held back a sigh. "Hey, can we listen to some music? Matt said they have radio stations here."

"Yep." Trace turned the knob and a country song blasted from the speakers. He lowered the volume. "We'll have reception for about thirty minutes. Go ahead, find something you like."

Thank God. She was sick of all the country music people played at the bar. After a few seconds of button pushing, she settled on a classic rock station. "This okay with you?" She looked over to find him smiling. "What?"

"I do enjoy your enthusiasm."

She thought for a moment and laughed. "Matt wanted to kill me by the time we reached Blackfoot Falls. On the trip back we had rules about how many times I was allowed to change stations."

Trace's grin widened. "No rules in this truck. Go for it."

"Ah, you really know how to sweet-talk a girl." She turned to face him and curled up in the seat. She wasn't the type to daydream or replay events over and over in her head, not since she was a teenager, anyway. But tonight would live in her memory for a very long time.

They'd been driving awhile when Trace flipped on the interior light and looked over at her.

She blinked. "What are you doing?"

"Getting another eyeful of that dress. Kind of a shame it has to come off," he said, watching her carefully.

Her breath caught. "And that would be…when?"

12

"This isn't how I planned tonight." He shook his head at himself. She was staring at him, looking as confused as he felt. "I want you, Nikki. That's not news, I know. But I swear I had every intention of taking the evening nice and slow...have dinner, show you around...return you to the Lone Wolf..."

"You do realize we left Kalispell a while ago." A small smile lifted her lips and made her eyes sparkle.

"Of course I know." He tried not to sound irritable. "I had to get us out of town before we passed one more damn motel and I did something stupid."

Laughing softly, she scooted closer. "I was really hoping for stupid."

His heart worked overtime. "Yeah?"

Nodding, she slid her palm up his thigh.

He checked the rearview mirror, saw there were no other cars and slowed to make a U-turn.

"Wait."

No way he'd misread her. But he brought the truck to a complete stop and met her eyes.

"Are we closer to Kalispell or Blackfoot Falls?"

"About the same. Maybe five minutes less to get home." He saw where she was headed with this. "No privacy, though."

She stroked his thigh, her heat penetrating the thick denim. The side of her hand brushed his fly, and he gritted his teeth. "Five minutes will seem like forever," she said, leaning over and kissing him. "And I bet we find lots of privacy."

"Not if you want a bed," he said, but he'd already released the brakes and was picking up speed toward Blackfoot Falls.

"You have a blanket in that big cargo box you keep in the back?" She reached up to flip off the light, letting her breast graze his arm.

Trace's laugh came out hoarse. "You're killing me."

"Sorry." Sighing, she laid her head on his shoulder. "Can't this truck go any faster?"

Later he'd be pissed at himself for stepping on the gas and ignoring caution. But right now he was thinking like her. The sooner they got to Blackfoot Falls the better, and he knew the perfect place. Pretty sad that at twenty-seven he'd resort to his high school make-out spot. Though no sense wasting a full moon.

He blasted the radio for a distraction. Then alternated between five and fifteen miles over the speed limit. By the time he turned off the highway and parked the truck, Nikki was pulling his shirt out of his jeans. She attacked the buttons, and man, he thought for sure she'd end up ripping the shirt open. But when he held her face in his hands and kissed her long and slow, her feverish pace settled to a sexy caress.

"You can wait here while I get the blanket and a flashlight from the back." He'd meant to pull away and go do what he said he'd do, but her eagerness was contagious. Barely had he dragged his lips from hers when his craving for more pulled him back for another sweep of her mouth.

She clung to his right shoulder, the tips of her fingers digging into him, her mouth soft and yielding, her exotic scent seeking a permanent nook inside his head. Damned if he knew how he could make himself leave her even for a minute. He cupped a hand over her breast. She wasn't wearing a bra and he felt her hard beaded nipple through the thin fabric.

Her fingers went back to the buttons and she continued where she'd left off, tugging with impatience, her breaths coming fast and hard in his mouth. Fear that he'd end up coming before he peeled off his jeans motivated him to make the break.

"Nikki, wait. Let me get us set up."

"I can't wait," she whispered, pushing his shirt off one shoulder and pressing her lips against his skin.

"I'm in the same boat, honey," he murmured, his body so tense he thought he might have to physically remove her to a safe distance. Her hand lowered to his fly. "Dammit, Nikki."

"Okay." She slumped back. "Hurry."

Leaving on the headlights, he fumbled with the door handle, cussing while she laughed. He waited until he was outside the truck before he looked at her. Nikki stared back, her moist lips glistening, her face flushed with need. "Your dress...don't take it off yet." He couldn't decide if he wanted to do the honors, or lie back and watch her strip down in the moonlight.

Her lips moved in a teasing smile. "You sure?"

"No." Barely intelligible, the strangled sound seemed to come from his throat. "Just...just leave it on for now."

He found the blanket, then remembered the flashlight was in his glove box. It didn't matter. The moon was bright and the sky cloudless. He inspected the tall grass, kicked away a couple rocks, then shook out the blanket. Crouching, he ran his palm over the wool to make sure nothing hard lay underneath, wishing he were about to make love to her on a soft bed with silk sheets.

Maybe he should've insisted they return to Kalispell. He should've taken a minute to make sure it was his brain doing the thinking. He didn't want to get this wrong. Nikki deserved to feel special. She'd nearly torn his heart out telling him about the prom incident and that prick Garrett.

He was straightening when he heard the car door. She stepped out and walked over to him. "I thought you'd started without me," she said, grinning and kicking her strappy black high heels onto the blanket.

"I like those." Nodding at the sandals, he loosened his buckle. "I like them a lot."

"You would. They're ridiculously high and pinch my feet."

"So why wear 'em?"

Nikki wrinkled her nose. "I knew you'd like them," she said, looking small and fragile in her bare feet. Her sudden burst of laughter had a nice sound to it, lusty and full of humor, and she wasn't the least self-conscious.

So far that's what he'd liked most about the night. Their relationship had reached a new level. Knowing she was comfortable enough with him to share a part of herself gave him a quiet pleasure he scarcely understood. It wasn't easy for a woman like her to let her guard down and trust she wouldn't be burned.

"What's that expression for?" Her smile slipped. "I was loud, I know." She shivered, her dark eyes sweeping a gaze toward the trees that flanked them on the right. "I hope I didn't attract a bunch of critters."

"Just one." He reached for her and tugged her close.

A warm gentle breeze stirred her hair as she tipped her head back to look up at him. "I love tonight. I love everything about it." She wound her arms around him. "And as much as I'm beginning to like Gypsy, I'm glad she stayed home."

"I wondered if you recognized the place."

"Of course I do. We kissed here for the first time."

Trace smiled. Damn sentimental coming from her. "We have a lot more to do than kissing." He skimmed his hand down her back, molded his palm and fingers over her firm round bottom. "After tonight, I suspect this place will deserve its own monument."

"Wow, that's pretty cocky."

"Hell no, I'm counting on you to do your part."

Her throaty laugh had him searching for her zipper. He found the tab and carefully drew it down her back. She did a little shimmy that helped him pull the snug-fitting dress up to her waist, then she raised her arms. His heart raced and his pulse was going nuts as he lifted the dress over her head. She stood there in nothing but tiny black panties.

He rearranged the long dark hair swirling around her shoulders so that he could see all of her. She had amazing skin, the slight golden color, the silky texture, her dusky rose nipples flushed with arousal… She was so beautiful he couldn't breathe. "God, Nikki."

"Come on, Trace," she said, putting her hands on his chest where his shirt hung open. She slid them up over his ribs and pecs and shoved the fabric off his shoulders.

He shrugged out of the shirt while she unzipped his fly, his short jerky movements hindering rather than speeding things along. "Wait," he said when she started tugging down his jeans. "I gotta get rid of the boots first."

"I'm not waiting." Her impatient hands were everywhere. But it was the one she was trying to slide into his boxers that would be his undoing.

"Okay, if that's how you want to play it." He took her shoulders and turned her around, ignoring her gasp, and forcing her to lean back against his chest and thighs. Banding an arm across her ribs, he held her in place and slipped his free hand inside her panties.

A FIERCE JOLT of longing rocked Nikki against his probing fingers. "What are you doing?" A moan punctuated her protest. His mouth was near her ear, his warm breath gliding over her sensitive skin. She clutched his forearm, intending to force him to let go, but all she did was hang on.

"You're so wet," he murmured, his voice a gravelly whisper, and then he was kissing the side of her neck and if he said anything else she couldn't hear, not when his fingers circled and plunged and made it hard for her to breathe.

She had the vague thought that she should make him stop. Need burned too hot inside her and it had been so long since she'd been with a man. And to make things worse and better at the same time, this was Trace.

God, he had great hands. She leaned back against his strong chest and closed her eyes, moaning when he cupped the weight of her breast. It took her a moment to realize that with both hands busy he was no longer trapping her body against his. But as soon as she tried to move, he released her breast and again banded his arm across her ribs. His fingers between her thighs hadn't let up even a little.

"Let me take your jeans off," she said, her voice a notch above a whisper.

In answer he intensified the pressure of his circling thumb on just the right spot to keep her submissive. The strength to argue was slipping away, replaced with an overwhelming need to let him take her to that surreal place where she couldn't think. Only feel the amazing things he was doing to her body. And knowing that if her weakened knees gave out, Trace was a man she could count on. He would never let her fall.

His sure and unrelenting fingers hit a new plateau, and the sound that escaped her lips was more whimper than moan. Heat surged through her, melting her bones and willpower and the last of her resistance.

"Come on, baby, let go," Trace whispered. "I've got you." His warm lips moved over her skin, down the side of her neck and brushed her shoulder.

She quivered, knowing it was coming, any second…any second…any…

Her climax hit with such force she rocked back against him. Still he wouldn't let up on the pressure. He tightened his hold around her middle, his other hand anchored between her thighs, his fingers steady and determined as the most breathtaking sensation rippled through her. Each new wave of pleasure pulled her in deeper, surrounding her in a soft sensual fog and threatening to rob her of air.

His breathing came as fast as hers, racing over her fevered skin, making her want more and more. Wanting him to share the same dizzying experience. She was still weak but able to stand on her own. He didn't fight her when she pried his arm away from her body, then moved her hips to disengage his fingers. She spun to face him and saw the desire burning hot in his eyes. She had the distinct feeling her stamina would be tested tonight. Well, she planned on testing his right back.

She went for his jeans again, but Trace seemed set on kissing her. He used his tongue to part her lips, then slipped inside her mouth and palmed her left breast. Nikki managed to shove his jeans down to the lower section of his thighs, and then she remembered his boots. That's what had tripped them up the first time.

Her patience was gone. She broke away. "Sit down."

"In a minute," he murmured, trying to capture her mouth again.

She turned her head, but that didn't stop him. He settled for kissing her jaw. "Now," she ordered, then gasped when he sucked in her nipple. She let him have his way for a few more seconds because, God, it felt so good. Then she lowered herself to the blanket and he followed her down.

"Boots," she said, shoving him away when he tried to lay her back. She grabbed one, and he tugged off the other boot.

After that it was easy to strip him of his jeans. She reached for his black boxers at the same time he tried to pull off her panties. They got tangled up for a second and started laughing, though neither of them would give in and let go. Finally they were both naked, and Nikki just stared at him.

How could he be so perfect? From the breadth of his shoulders to the thickness and length of his erection, to the ridges of muscle in his thighs and calves. She wanted him to stand up so she could get a better look. And his ass…she'd already felt it through the denim and knew it was perfect, too. She still wanted to see.

"I don't suppose you'd want to get up and twirl around for me?" she said, grinning at how his brows shot up.

"Not as long as you're willing to reciprocate." His slow sexy smile distracted her.

She jerked at the feel of his hand sliding between her thighs. Clamping her legs together she stopped him from going any further. "Condoms? We should be ready."

"Right here." He reached behind to his jeans and produced a packet.

"Wow, you're good. I didn't even see you—" She'd forgotten about his hand. The startling invasion of his fingers made her tremble. She bit down on her lip, too hard, but at least it brought her to her senses. "No," she said, wiggling backward. "Not yet."

She came up on her knees and pushed on his shoulders, forcing him to lie back. He wouldn't go down all the way, but braced himself on his elbows and watched her. She didn't care. She had what she wanted. With the tip of her finger she lightly traced the hard silken length of his cock, then circled the crown. It leaped at her touch.

"This isn't gonna work." His voice was hoarse and his expression strained. His body had tightened, so that it seemed every muscle across his belly and down his thighs was clearly defined.

"Seems to be working just fine." Nikki gave him a light squeeze then stroked upward.

His laugh turned into a groan. He briefly closed his eyes and clenched his jaw. Then he let out a slow exhale. "I'm serious."

"About?" She took her time exploring, grateful for the bright moonlight, and ignoring his low moans, the occasional hiss. She already knew from the day he was at the Lone Wolf that his belly, shoulders and back were as tan as his forearms and face. He obviously worked a lot without a shirt. But now she also knew exactly how low he wore his jeans. The tan stopped two inches below his belly button. Still, he wasn't lily-white, and she wondered if the McAllisters had Native American blood in them.

"Nikki." He grabbed her wrist and moved her hand away while raising himself to a sitting position.

"I'm not done."

Curling his fingers around her nape, he pulled her face toward his until he'd claimed her lips. The kiss wasn't rough but neither was it anywhere close to gentle. It felt to Nikki as if a fair amount of restraint was required for him to keep himself in check.

With his other hand, he found her breast and toyed with the nipple. She was sensitive there, always had been, but Trace doing the touching made her tremble like a butterfly caught in a windstorm. He switched to her other breast, then kissed his way down from her chin to her collarbone to the nipple he'd abandoned. She watched him take the pearled tip into his mouth, sucking greedily for a few seconds, then lightly flicking it with his tongue.

She let her eyes drift closed and arched against him. "I want you inside me," she whispered.

His fingers tightened on her neck, the slight pressure an amazing turn-on, even as his mouth stilled. She could feel his breath, though, warm and moist and seductive, skimming her hypersensitive flesh. He pressed a final kiss to her breast, released her neck and urged her to lie back.

He knelt beside her to tear open the packet, recoiling when she touched his erection. "Not a good idea."

"Really?"

His laugh came out shaky. "Really." He sheathed himself, then spread her legs farther apart.

She wanted to touch him so very badly but the desperate need to feel him hot and throbbing inside her won out. He positioned himself between her thighs, running his hands along the outside all the way to her calves, catching an ankle and bending her leg. He paused to kiss the tender skin just above her knee, and her impatience flared.

Yes, it felt good, but she wanted him pushing inside and filling her to the hilt. The need was so great it was crazy, completely irrational, igniting sparks of both longing and panic she didn't understand.

He pulled her legs around his waist, and she lifted her hips and clutched two fistfuls of the wool blanket. The big bright moon was behind him so she couldn't see his face. It didn't seem fair that he could see hers.

"God, look at you," he murmured, and teased her opening with his cock. He'd barely dipped inside when he leaned back again.

"Dammit, Trace."

"Don't you want this to last?"

"No. Later, yes." She probably wasn't making any sense. Too bad. "Now, no. Come on. Please."

He moaned her name and plunged inside her. The force behind his entry shocked her even though it was exactly what she wanted. She couldn't catch her breath. Couldn't form the words to tell him to keep going when he slid partway out. But he knew and pushed back in, slower now, but just as deep.

She tightened her legs around him, clenched his cock, daring him to withdraw.

Trace shuddered. "I can't hold back."

"I don't want you to."

He surprised her by pulling out. The next thrust nearly rocked her senseless. She let go of the blanket. It wouldn't help her. Instead she clung to him, lifting her hips to meet each thrust, the fire raging inside her growing out of control.

"Open your eyes, Nikki," he whispered, still gripping her hips, but the pressure of his fingertips easing.

She lifted her lashes. Even though his face was in shadow, she sensed he was staring into her eyes. The thrusts had subsided, too, but he was still moving inside her as he lowered his head and kissed her parted lips. At this new angle, his erection sent a jolt of sensation that shimmered through her entire body.

Trace stopped moving. The earthy cry that exploded from his throat raced along her nerve endings. It seemed impossible that she could be triggered by a sound, but the climax that washed over her was stunningly real. So was the hot openmouthed kiss consuming her.

It struck her as funny that he could be kissing her with this much hunger, as if she was the first woman he'd encountered after being celibate for a year. She knew that wasn't true.

He lifted his head. "You're laughing?"

"No. Uh-uh." She bit her lip. "Just a little."

After a long silence, he said, "I'm gonna need some serious therapy."

"No, you don't." Nikki giggled and hugged him. "I'm not laughing at *that* part."

Bracing himself on one elbow, he tenderly brushed aside the strands of hair that clung to her cheek. "Will I hate myself for asking?"

She heard the smile in his voice and decided she needed to see his face. "Roll over," she said, giving him a gentle shove.

He did, and took her with him.

Soft moonlight lit his features. Much better. Sighing happily, she stacked her hands on his chest, rested her chin on them and stared into his darkened eyes. "Am I too heavy?"

"Not even a tiny bit."

"Good answer." She shivered when he cupped her backside with his large callused hands. He looked serious. "What are you thinking about?"

A faint smile curved his mouth. "I knew from the get-go that you, Nikki Flores, were gonna be a heap of trouble."

13

"WHAT DID YOU DREAM about, Nikki?" Trace asked out of the blue. He shifted his gaze from the glowing moon and stars shining against the dark sky to her face. "When you were a kid, what did you want to be or do?"

She lay beside him on the blanket, both of them looking up at the stars, completely naked. Her left palm was pressed to his right palm, their fingers intertwined. "When I was really little, like second or third grade, I wanted to be an astronaut."

"A what?"

"Hey. It could've happened."

"I'm sure you could be anything you set your mind to. It just wasn't what I expected, is all."

"Remember I lived in Houston. NASA wasn't far and was always in the news. Turns out I didn't really want to be an astronaut," she admitted. "I thought if I had a big important job, then my father would love me."

Trace touched her cheek. "He didn't even deserve you."

She smiled, shrugging. "I guess every kid with divorced parents or who was abandoned has an 'if only' version floating around in their heads. It's no big deal."

"I reckon you're right. Even after my dad died I kept thinking if only I hadn't argued with him over that stupid dance…"

"You don't still go there, do you?"

"No, not for a long time. We had a great relationship and I focus on that."

She squeezed his hand. "Look at my poor brother. After all he went through he never completely let go of wanting to please Wallace. In February Matt found a stack of articles going back to the beginning of his rodeo career. They were hidden in Wallace's desk, but did he have the decency to say a word to Matt?"

Nikki breathed in the fresh Montana air, unwilling to let the old man ruin her night. He was gone and couldn't hurt them anymore. Unless she allowed it.

Trace shifted so that he could put an arm around her, providing a nice comfy spot for her head to lay on his shoulder.

"You know what, though…? I scored because I ended up with having Matt for a brother. I'd trade a father for him any day."

"Matt's a good guy. I'm glad for both you and my sister." He kissed her hair, then smiled at her. "I'm not doing too badly, either."

He did look happy.

But for how long?

The unwelcome thought sneaked in before she could block it. Tonight was about tonight, and that was it. One brief moment in the whole scheme of things. They'd had sex, so what? She'd only hurt herself if she started confusing hormones and unjustified feelings for Trace with a future that would magically fall into place.

"So," he said, "once you nixed the rocketing into space thing, what then? What did little Nikki have a hankering for?"

She sighed. "Little naive Nikki woke up and figured out dreaming was for fools or people who had time and money to spend."

"Come on now, you don't mean that."

"I do," she said with a laugh, mainly to tone down her pessimistic words. "What about you? What haunted your dreams?"

"Haunted, huh?" He rested a cupped hand on her breast. Somehow instead of being suggestive, it was a casual, comfortable touch. Still, it made her pulse race. "In eighth grade," he said, "I decided I wanted to go to college and study modern ranching techniques."

"Did you?" she asked, and he shook his head. "Why not? Rachel and Jesse went."

"Lack of money and bad timing."

She pulled back to look at him, then found a position lying on her side that made it easier to watch his face. The Sundance was the second largest ranch in the county. The Lone Wolf beat them by only a hundred acres. She'd figured the new dude ranch operation was helping to bring in cash, but mostly to avoid layoffs while times were tough. At least that had been her assumption. It was hard to imagine the McAllister family having serious money problems. Severe enough that Trace couldn't afford school.

"What do you mean by bad timing?" She decided to lead with the less touchy issue.

"After Jesse finished college he joined the air force. None of us expected that. My father had passed away two years earlier and Cole was running the ranch. He did a hell of a job. I helped as much as I could but I was still wet behind the ears. Man, I would've felt like shit taking off for college and leaving him to shoulder everything. I figured I still had time, even if I had to wait until Jesse got out of the military." He lifted a thick lock of her hair, then watched it sift through his fingers and fall behind her shoulder.

She thought the gesture sweet until she realized he was simply preserving his view of her bare breast. It made her smile.

"What?"

"Nothing." She scooted closer and rested her hand on his waist. "And?"

"Rachel was coming up behind me and I knew she was itching to go to that fancy college in Dallas. Tuition wasn't cheap, although we didn't have money problems back then. Several years later, yeah, big hurdle. But nearly everyone around here was in the same fix, and we're still meeting payroll so no complaints from me."

"Except Jesse is home now and you should be able to go to school if you want."

"Money is still tight. Anyway, no point in learning about a bunch of new techniques we don't have the financial resources to implement. Maybe someday." He shrugged a shoulder. "I read a lot and try to keep up on what's out there or what might be coming down the chute. Let everybody else be guinea pigs."

She hated that he'd been held back, and was stunned to learn the McAllisters weren't the family of power and means she'd imagined. They'd compromised and worked their butts off so their hired hands could keep their jobs. She liked them all the more.

"By the way..." Trace let the backs of his fingers trail over her breast. Her nipple's instant response made his mouth curve in a smile. "Don't say anything about my wanting to go to college to anybody. No need kicking up dust for nothing."

"Doesn't your mom or any of your family know?"

"Nope. I was a pretty decent student. I got mostly B's, though, not like Rachel and Jesse. My mom was still mourning my dad, and I think she figured I was more like Cole and didn't have a head for school."

"You must've mentioned it at some point."

He leaned closer and tongued her nipple. They'd already made love twice in the three hours since returning from Kalispell. Trace had been quick to inform her he had a third condom in his glove box. She knew he wanted to distract her, but he also wanted her, period. No hiding that fact with his hard-on swelling hot and thick between them.

She touched him, hadn't yet wrapped her fingers around his penis when he jerked back.

"Careful now, honey, or we'll be heading for that finish line too soon again."

"We?" Nikki laughed. "You're like a teenager. You can't hold back for one—" She gasped at the speed with which he spread her legs and positioned himself between them.

He pressed soft warm kisses just under her belly button, down to the narrow strip of hair left from her Brazilian wax.

"Hey." Ordering herself not to react, she arched off the blanket anyway. "We were talking."

"Go right ahead." He slid a hand under her butt and lightly squeezed.

She tried to grab a fistful of hair but missed. He'd moved out of reach, trailing his lips lower, inserting a finger to test how slick she'd grown. He lifted his head, and her groan turned into a laugh at his self-satisfied smirk. "What are you doing?"

His gaze moved to her breasts. Looking like a kid who'd been told not to touch the hot stove but couldn't seem to help himself, he rubbed his thumb over her nipple. "You haven't figured it out yet?"

"I know *what* you're doing. What I want to know is— Oh." She jumped at the intimate swipe of his tongue.

Trace licked his way back up to her lower belly and smiled. "I'm gonna go so slow you'll be begging me to hurry."

IT WAS AFTER FOUR by the time Trace drove her to the house. The foyer lamp had been left on, as well as the porch light. Matt's room was completely dark. He normally didn't stay up too late, though she doubted he ever fell asleep before she got home from the Watering Hole. She wondered if he'd been listening for her tonight.

Trace surprised her by cutting the engine. She'd been ready to jump out and dash inside before the hands' two Border collies started barking.

"I'm not making out with you in front of the house," she said, barely able to keep a straight face.

"You don't think I could get you to do that if I wanted?"

Her startled laugh came out much too loud and she covered her mouth. "You cocky bastard."

"Come here." He reached for her, catching an arm and pulling her toward him.

"Oh, no. You don't even get a good-night kiss for that."

He settled for holding her hand. "We should talk."

Her heart nose-dived. "About?"

"How we should handle our relationship."

Relationship. She turned the word over in her mind. They'd had sex, and yes, it was really great sex. The best she'd ever had, and she hoped for more of it. But that didn't mean anything had changed between them.

"I'm not sure how open you want to be about us," he said. "There are things to consider."

"I'm not going to take out an ad in the *Salina Gazette* and announce I had sex with you, if that's what you're worried about."

"Nikki." He looked shocked, his hand tightening around hers. "Did I really give you that impression?"

"No. I'm sorry." She sighed. "I promise we aren't pulling anything over on Matt. I doubt he thinks we've been playing checkers all night. Personally, I don't care that he knows we've had sex."

For a moment she thought Trace might've flinched slightly. He continued to study her, his expression troubled. The silence kept growing, and she didn't know how to fill it. He hadn't released her hand but whether he did or not, in a second she was getting out of the truck.

"I'll talk to Matt later," he said, finally. "Tell him it was my fault…that I kept you out late."

"You will not. I can't believe you—Matt is my brother, not my guardian. For God's sake, Trace, I'm twenty-five." She really wanted to throw something. "I can handle my own life. God," she said through gritted teeth.

Trace just sat there as the furrow in his brow deepened. "That came out wrong. I only meant that I don't want him thinking that anyone saw us, or— Look, this is a small town, people talk. He should know we were careful. That's all I'm saying."

"Careful about what? Are you worried about my reputation?"

"Well, yeah. You know how bad the gossip can be."

She breathed in deeply. First, he talked about a relationship, and now he cared if anyone had seen them? That didn't even make sense. She might be Matt's sister, but everyone knew she wasn't like him.

Though she *would* prefer not to be thought of as just another notch on Trace's belt once he moved on, but if that happened… "If there's gossip, I'll deal with it."

"Just you? On your own?"

She nodded. "Seriously. Don't worry about it. I can take the heat."

"Honey, do you regret what we did tonight?"

"No. Not at all." Nikki sighed. "I really don't. I just hope things don't change between us."

Trace stayed silent for a long time. He'd turned his head so that he could stare out the windshield and into the darkness.

"Hey," she said, and he turned back. "If we hook up again,

we hook up again. If we don't, that's okay." She shrugged. "That's all."

If he'd seemed confused before, now he looked pissed. "What?"

"Nothing. You seem to have figured it all out." He pushed his hand through his hair. "Look, you're strong and independent and I admire that about you. I have no doubt you can handle your life just fine. But that doesn't mean I'll sit on my thumbs and not want to have your back. If it makes it easier letting Matt know what's what, then I want to be there."

Again, she didn't know what to say. With the exception of her mother and now Matt, no one had ever had her back. Not in the way Trace meant. It seemed hard to believe he was sincere, but everything from the way he looked at her to the care he took when he held her said he was.

That didn't mean she thought he'd still be knocking on her door next week. "Fine."

"Damn right it's fine." He cupped her chin and looked into her eyes. "Tell me you wouldn't be there for me."

"Of course I would," she murmured, still not sure how to take this. She'd expected him to be the one to make it clear there were no strings attached. In her experience guys tended to do that after they got what they wanted. Maybe their friendship made things different.

She'd never been friends with a guy before. Garret had been concerned with his own reputation, not hers. And the others? She doubted if they'd ever given it one thought. All Trace did was confuse her. "I'd better get inside before the dogs start barking." She lifted the handle, but before she could get out, Trace had come around to her side.

"What?"

"You couldn't wait and let me get the door for you?"

Nikki grinned. "First you say sexist things about showing me off and then you want to open the door for me."

"At least I'm consistent." That damn smile of his. He slid his arms around her, apparently unconcerned that the porch light was shining on them. "I want that good-night kiss."

She glanced at the dark bunkhouse. "So much for not sparking any gossip."

"Yeah," he said, pulling away a bit. He rubbed her back, brushed a quick kiss on the tip of her nose. "About that…I sure can try to keep us low-key, but it means I'd have to stay away from the Watering Hole." His gaze dropped to her mouth. "Although I don't see me pulling it off for more than an hour."

"A whole hour, huh?" Nikki was getting pretty good at appearing cool, except for her traitorous sprinting pulse. "You better not be using me to discourage all those women from chasing after you."

"Using you? You know better." He tipped her chin up. "Gotta admit, though, that's a nice bonus." He looked at her as if kissing her this very instant was the most important thing in his whole life. But he held back. For her. When he let go of her hand to step away, she grabbed on to his shirtsleeve.

"Wait." Why she had the sudden urge to confess, she didn't know. But she had to tell him about the prom dress. She had to say it out loud because remembering had triggered old shame that started eating at her on the way home. And Trace was her friend, right? She hoped he wouldn't judge. If he did, well, still better to let him see her for who she was. "I have something to tell you."

He nodded, his gaze narrowing slightly.

"That dress…the one my mom bought me for the prom. It cost so much, I had no business asking for it in the first place." She paused to swallow. "I'd picked it up from the store just before Garrett cancelled on me. I should've turned around right then and gotten a refund. But I was furious and hurt and I wasn't thinking."

She shook her head, amazed that the pain of that day felt

so fresh. Almost as crippling as her shame. "I missed the bus and had to walk home. The dress was wrapped in plastic but I'd dragged it a mile before I saw that the hem had been completely ruined. My mother had worked so many hours so she could get me that dress."

Staring at him, she let out a pent-up breath. Well crap, confessing hadn't felt as freeing as she'd hoped. Probably because he didn't really understand what it had been like for her and her mother back then. Which was made more clear by his helpless shrug.

"Hey, fifteen. That's a tough age. Everybody messes up when they're fifteen."

"But I hurt my mom, the only one who's always been there for me. What kind of person does that?"

"A teenager." He'd gone back to rubbing her back. "Feel better getting it off your chest?"

"I'm not sure," she said, still off balance and mentally scrambling to pull herself back on track.

Trace talked as if what she'd done was nothing. Like skipping a class or not returning a library book. He'd implied there would be more between them. He'd used the word *relationship,* although she'd have to ask him what he meant by that. Later. Because she wasn't certain she wanted to know yet. There was a part of her that wanted to pretend that the look in his eyes was full of promises he'd keep. But that couldn't be true. She wasn't some delicate flower. She'd never be that. No matter where she lived, or how clean her slate was supposed to be.

"Come on," he said. "Let's get you to the door. I've kept you out way past your bedtime." His arm was around her back as he led her up the steps. "Besides, if we get close enough to the door, I don't think anyone could see me steal one more kiss."

She didn't object. And when he kissed her in the shadows,

she kissed him back. But instead of getting swept away by the kiss, an unpleasant thought occurred to her. Had she really needed to tell him about the dress? Or was she trying to sabotage the best thing that had ever happened to her? It didn't matter, though.

Whatever this was between them would come to an end sooner or later. Given her experiences, she'd bet on sooner.

TRYING TO WAKE UP, Nikki stared at the coffee carafe, watching the brew drip, and yawning as if she hadn't slept in a month. The clock taunted her, claiming it was one-thirty in the afternoon, but her poor tired body and pounding head swore it was the middle of the night. That was more accurate since she hadn't fallen asleep until after seven.

As soon as there was enough coffee brewed, she filled a mug before returning the carafe to the fancy chrome station so it could finish the job. She savored the first sip, convinced there wasn't enough caffeine in the house to get her moving faster.

Naturally tonight she had to work. With it being her first day back since Wallace had died, she hoped people gave her space. She didn't need it because of his death, but she was bound to be cranky from too little sleep.

"Hey, you made coffee." Matt entered the kitchen from outside. She hadn't even heard the door. "You just get up? Late night?" He tried to look innocent, but she saw the corners of his mouth quirk up.

"Not particularly." She wasn't volunteering a damn thing.

He brought a mug out from the upper cabinet, then opened the fridge. "We have to talk about Lucy."

"What about her?"

"Did she say anything to you about staying on here?"

"Oh." Nikki saw why he'd brought up the subject. The refrigerator shelves were sparse. "No, but I think she would've talked to you before me."

"The past few days seemed to fly by. I don't know if she needs the money or would rather quit working."

"I can run to town and pick up groceries." She noticed the wood floor needed sweeping. God, she hoped Lucy stayed on. It was a big house. "I'll sweep and dust later. Right now coffee isn't optional."

"I won't be surprised if she wants out. She's getting up there in years and I wouldn't want her doing too much. If she's ready to retire we'll find someone to come in a couple times a week."

Nikki leaned a hip against the counter. "I'll chip in to cover the cost."

"No, you won't. A housekeeper's salary comes out of the ranch fund. It's half yours, anyway."

"I'm not arguing with you over the Lone Wolf again. I don't want anything from Wallace."

"Don't be so damn hardheaded." Matt set down his mug with a thud. "This place was never Wallace's to give. How many more times do I have to explain the Gunderson trust fund to you?"

"None." Nikki topped off her coffee. She was going to the living room to drink it in peace.

"Fine. I'll let the attorney spell out the terms for you. Maybe he can get through that thick skull of yours."

"Good luck with that." She had no intention of being railroaded into going to an attorney's office.

"Tomorrow morning I'm flying to Dallas. Just overnight. I'll be back by noon the following day. Mr. Kessler will meet us here at 4:00 p.m. to read the will."

She sighed. So much for refusing to go to the attorney's office. "Wait." She stopped at the door and turned. "Did you say Dallas?" she asked, and he nodded. "For a rodeo?"

"No. Not until next month. I'm meeting with a guy who breeds champion bulls. The Lone Wolf is doing fine for now but we have to keep our eye on the future."

Ranch business wasn't on her mind. Having the house to herself overnight? Different story. "Sounds like a short trip. Are you sure you won't need to stay longer?"

"You're not afraid to stay here alone, are you?" Matt didn't bother to hide his grin. "I'm sure Trace wouldn't mind baby-sitting."

"Oh, shut up." She left the kitchen smiling, too, thinking how it would've been just like this ten years ago had they known each other. He would've teased her all the time, and she wouldn't have liked it. She did now.

She headed for the privacy of the living room, one hand searching her jeans' pocket for her phone. This was awesome. If she could get Sheila or Gretchen to work for her tomorrow night, it would be even more perfect.

"Nikki?" Matt had followed her as far as the foyer. "Don't forget our appointment with Mr. Kessler. He's driving in from Kalispell."

"No reason for me to be here."

"You're specifically named in his will."

She fisted her hand around the cell phone. "I already told you…I don't want anything from that man."

"Fine. Whatever he's left you, give it to charity. I don't care." He raked a hand through his hair and heaved a tired sigh. "Just be here on Wednesday."

14

TRACE OPENED HIS EYES, stretched out his arms while arching his back, then rolled over and cussed a blue streak when he saw the digital clock. How could it be 1:40 in the morning?

"Son of a bitch."

He jumped out of bed and grabbed the clean pair of jeans he'd left on his dresser. Before he pulled them on he figured he'd better make a pit stop and ducked into his attached bathroom. He'd showered and changed his boxers earlier after quitting work for the day. Dark stubble covered his jaw and chin but he'd purposely left shaving for the last minute.

His razor wasn't where it should be. That's right. He'd abandoned it where he stood this morning the instant he remembered to replace the condoms in his wallet, just before he'd had to haul his ass to work. He found the razor next to the tube of hand lotion he'd bought to help with his calluses. Then grabbed the can of shaving cream and was about to lather up when it finally hit him. He was rushing for nothing. The Watering Hole was closed and Nikki would've driven home by now. She could be sound asleep at this point.

Part of him hoped she was since she'd told him she hadn't gone to bed until seven this—well, yesterday—morning. The selfish part still wanted to curse and punch walls. How could he have overslept? He'd even set the alarm. Yeah, right, getting only three hours after dropping her off had nothing to do with it.

After supper he'd lain down for a two-hour nap, mostly because Nikki had made him promise. Her concern hadn't been misplaced. He'd spent a good portion of the day branding, a job he disliked when he wasn't tired. Today had been a mother, chasing and wrestling calves until he couldn't tell where one ache in his back ended and the next one started. It would've been irresponsible of him to drive to town that exhausted. But he'd wanted to see her. He still did, but he wouldn't be a jerk about it.

Maybe he could at least call her. If she was asleep her phone would be off or charging. If not, he could explain why he hadn't shown up. Though she'd practically begged him to stay home and hit the sack early. Tomorrow Matt would be in Dallas and they had the whole house to themselves. He grinned just thinking about how excited she'd sounded when she told him. It had been kind of a relief. Nikki wasn't always easy to read.

That conversation in the car when he'd dropped her off had played and replayed every minute he'd had a breather. He hated her casual talk of hooking up, how she'd been so determined he knew she didn't want anything serious.

He'd been hoping for more. It still bothered him that he hadn't said as much. But damn, how could he when he wasn't certain what he meant by *more?*

Oh, in his head he was real clear he didn't want her seeing anyone else, and that he only had eyes for Nikki. But coming right out and asking her to be his girlfriend? That was tricky. Especially when so much was going on in her life.

Then there were his own doubts. She wasn't like anyone he'd ever known. Feisty as a wild colt, cagey about her feelings, and so damn beautiful it made him ache. She intrigued him as much as she rattled him. The combination had never been on his wish list, but now that he'd met her, other women had started fading into the background.

Maybe he should be more worried about himself and all the weird feelings he was experiencing but couldn't understand. And maybe he wasn't anxious to look too closely, either. Hell, he was only twenty-seven. Too young to be getting serious about a woman. Cole and Jesse had waited until they were in their thirties…

Screw it. He grabbed his phone off the dresser and hit speed dial. He had to try. Even if only to hear her voice. He'd lost track of the number of rings but was prepared to leave a message when she answered.

"Hey," she said. "You should be asleep."

"I was. I even set the alarm, then slept through it."

"Good."

"Thanks." He smiled at her sigh, then used his free hand to stack the pillows against the headboard of his king bed.

"You know what I meant so stop it."

"Sounds like you had a pleasant night at work."

"It was okay. A few customers mentioned the funeral or apologized for not coming, but overall it wasn't bad. I'm feeling icky about tomorrow night. I called Sheila, but she has plans and can't cover for me. I even called Gretchen, totally forgetting that she's pregnant. Can you believe that? I felt like an ass."

"Yeah, I believe it." Still in his boxers, he crawled into bed and lay back against the stacked pillows. "Today I almost branded Josh instead of a calf. He'll be telling that story for a while."

Nikki laughed. "I can't wait for tomorrow. I wish you were here now."

"Me, too. Want me to try climbing up to your bedroom window?"

"Um, you have experience doing that sort of thing?"

"No," he drawled out the word. "Not me. I'd rather charm my way in." His teasing was met with a long stretch of silence. "You know I'm joking, right?"

"Yes." She tried to brush it off with a laugh, but he knew he'd hit a nerve.

Trace scrubbed at his face. She'd seen him casually flirting with the guests, or more like humoring them when they flirted because lately he hadn't been into that whole thing. And God only knew what kind of stories she'd heard about him from Sam or any of the other guys who hung out at the Watering Hole. They could've said something jokingly not knowing it mattered. "You haven't told me what Matt said about our late night. He seem cool with it?"

She let out an exasperated sigh, which oddly made her sound more relaxed. "He asked if I needed you to babysit me while he's in Dallas."

Trace chuckled, relieved Matt could joke about it. "I guess we can assume Rachel knows, too. Unless you asked him to keep it quiet."

"I didn't say anything." She hesitated. "You could come over right now and spend the night and I wouldn't care who saw you. Rachel does it all the time. The only reason I won't let you is that you need your sleep."

He swung his legs out of bed, glancing at the clock, knowing he could be there by 2:10 a.m., five minutes later if he shaved first. "I got lots of sleep. Almost six hours."

"Not enough. I plan on totally wearing you out tomorrow night, or technically it's tonight. Hey, what are you doing? Sounds like you're—" Nikki's soft laugh was pure disbelief. "You are not driving over here."

"Come on now, you just said—"

"God, you can't be that horny. I'm sure you can wait a few more hours."

He entered the bathroom, his enthusiasm waning. Man, she really did think he was only in this for the sex. This was pretty messed up. He thought about how that boy Garrett had treated her and the strange *Salina Gazette* remark. Maybe it was time for him to man up, publicly claim her.

"Trace? You still there?"

"Yeah, sorry."

"I figured you fell asleep on me."

"Nah, just thinking." He rubbed his chest. "You're probably right, though. We should both get some rest. You said Matt's going to be in Dallas only one night?"

"He has to be back in time for the reading of Wallace's will," she muttered.

"I take it you have to be present."

"According to Matt, I do."

Trace decided to drop the subject. No use getting her riled. "Are you in bed now?"

"Yes. You?"

"I'll be crawling in between the sheets in two seconds." He turned off the bathroom light, picturing how she'd look with her silky dark hair spread out over a pillow. "Just so you know…I wasn't coming over for a booty call." He hesitated. Oh, hell, it wouldn't kill him to say the words. "I miss you, Nikki."

CUSTOMERS KEPT POURING in to the Watering Hole, which made the night go by quickly. But no way would Nikki be able to leave early. She might've been in a more pleasant mood if Trace had come to the bar to wait for her, but she was still glad she talked him into meeting her at the Lone Wolf. It turned out he was working late, anyway. He'd traded an early morning chore with one of the Sundance hands who wanted to play poker. That meant they could sleep in. He was going to need the rest, she thought, smiling. She hoped they both would.

"Glad to see you won't be a sourpuss again tonight." Sadie glanced at the order ticket Nikki set down along with her tray. "After being such a delight when you'd nagged me to let you come back to work."

"I haven't bitten off a single head yet, now have I?"

Grinning, Sadie grabbed bottles of tequila and whiskey and started pouring. "Heck, I just figured you being grouchy was on account of your trip to Kalispell, but I didn't want to say anything for fear of my life."

Nikki stared in astonishment. "How do you— No, you can't know."

Sadie laughed.

Nikki groaned. "This town is unreal…half the time I swear I'm being punked."

"Being what?"

The door opened, and Nikki turned to see who was coming to torment her now. Tall, lean, mid-to-late thirties, wearing faded jeans and boots like every other cowboy in the place… She didn't recognize him.

"Hell, look what the cat dragged in." Staring at the man, Sadie cocked her head to the side. "What are you doing around these parts? It can't be roundup time again."

His lazy smile disappeared in a flash. "Christ, Sadie, now you're gonna give me shit about that. And here I came in for a beer and a sympathetic ear."

"Since I don't know what on earth you're talking about, I have no response."

"Something slipped past you?" Nikki pretended to be shocked. "Wow. This has to be some kind of record."

Sadie narrowed her eyes. "Watch yourself, missy."

"Don't have to." Nikki smiled sweetly and picked up her tray. "It seems everyone else around here does it for me."

Sadie shook her head. "Aaron, this is Nikki, Matt Gunderson's sister. You know Matt, don't you?"

"Know of him, that's it." Touching the rim of his hat, Aaron gave Nikki a quick smile. "I was hoping I'd find Trace here," he said, glancing around. "Either of you seen him?"

"Not tonight." Sadie nodded at Nikki. "You must know where he is."

"Home."

Aaron gave her a closer look. "You expecting him here later?"

"No, he's working. Sorry, but I have drinks to deliver." She left with her tray, her mind racing. Whoever this guy was if he did anything to screw up their night she would just scream.

"What's Aaron doing here?" Eli Roscoe asked, when she dropped off his beer.

"I have no idea. Who is he?"

"A government guy…works for the Bureau of Land Management." The older man squinted under his bushy graying eyebrows. "He has something to do with rounding up mustangs living on public land. About the only time we see him around here is when he's looking for the McAllister boys to help."

Sitting across from Jerry at the next table, Chip said, "Too soon for another roundup, isn't it?"

"I ain't got an opinion on the matter," Eli said, "but I know Jesse McAllister thinks so, and I believe Trace is still straddling the fence on the issue. Says he's got more reading to do but my feeling is that he's got the same notion as Jesse. If Aaron's looking for their help, he's not gonna get it this time."

Nikki delivered more beers and shots, swinging around so she could keep an eye on Aaron. He was leaning on the bar, drinking from a mug and talking to Sadie.

"Just last week Trace told me he didn't think they've given the sterilization program enough time," Jerry said. "Infertility treatments were given to the Pryor Mountain horses along the Montana-Wyoming border. They're hoping that'll stabilize the size of the herd, but he said it's too soon to tell and we got no business removing horses until we know more."

"Hell, I'll admit I don't know crap about what's been going on," Chip added. "But I'll side with Trace. You know him, he's smart and always reading up on things. I've never known him to go in half-cocked on something."

Other customers who'd overheard the conversation weighed in, most of them agreeing it was too early for another roundup. What Nikki found fascinating was how much these men respected Trace's opinion, even the old-timers. They were interested in where Jesse stood as well, but that wasn't a surprise. He was older, more serious and well educated.

Trace was so laid-back, and seemed to cruise by on a shrug and a smile. But most of these people had known him his entire life. They'd watched him grow up, become a man, they knew there was substance behind the smile. When he had an opinion on something important, they took notice.

"What you damn fools are forgettin' is that the land is being overgrazed in the meantime, which means hungry animals." It was Sam's voice.

Nikki turned to see him coming from the back room with his empty mug. She really hadn't meant to ignore him or the others playing pool. The discussion had drawn her in.

His comment was met with general disgust.

"Trace said all that was taken into account when they thinned the herd and started the program." Chip glared straight at Sam. "You think for one minute Trace would let animals starve if he could help it?"

"What I think is that all you dumb bastards just love kissing McAllister ass. You sound like a bunch of little girls out here. Ooh," he mimicked, in a shrill tone, "Trace said this, Trace said that, Trace said I should go drown myself so I believe I will." He set his mug on Nikki's tray, and boy, did she get a whiff of his boozy breath. "It's damn pitiful," he added in his natural drawl, then winked. "I'll take another one, darlin'."

Her guilt over ignoring him vanished. "If you knew how much I want to pull out your lashes, one by one, every time you wink, you would stop." She narrowed her eyes. "Which is highly recommended in case that was too subtle or you're too dense."

She sidestepped him to check on the other pool players, not even smiling when everyone laughed.

"You boys hear that?" Sam said, spreading his hands. "She's crazy about me."

Nikki almost smiled then. She sighed instead. God, the man was like an untrained puppy—cute sometimes, but more often making you mad by peeing on the carpet. Or maybe that was giving him too much credit. She hurried to collect orders, hoping to squeeze in a minute to call Trace and warn him about Aaron, while Sadie poured beers and mixed drinks.

It was crazy how much pride she'd felt listening to these men talk about Trace. She had nothing to do with the respect he'd earned by being thoughtful and levelheaded. At the table behind Chip and Jerry, she overheard an older rancher tell his friend that since his son moved, Trace was the guy he knew he could count on in an emergency.

How horribly she'd misjudged him in February. Or had she really? She wasn't someone who shared easily. She certainly wasn't big on admitting her fears or the incredibly stupid choices of her youth, but she'd let her guard down with Trace, more than once. So something inside her was giving the green light. She just hoped it wasn't her heart getting confused. Falling for him would still be a mistake even if she did trust him.

This thing they had was fun, comfortable and exciting.

She'd like to believe it could last, but she knew better. She really needed to remember that. Easy to risk everything when you had nothing to lose. Loving then losing Trace? That could kill her.

He was sitting in his truck when she pulled up to the house. She parked her pickup behind him instead of her regular spot. They both climbed out at the same time.

"You boxing me in for a reason?" His teeth flashed in the bright moonlight as he walked toward her.

Had she remembered to leave the porch light on she'd be able to see that slow heart-stopping smile of his. "I don't want you running off before I'm done with you."

"Well now, that sounds promising." No hat tonight, which she was surprised to find she missed. The snug worn jeans made up for it. He stopped not three feet away and looked her up and down. "You went to work like that?"

"Um, yes." She glanced down at her usual jeans and stretchy blue V-neck top. "What's wrong?"

He made a sudden grab for her, scooping her up and making her squeal. "What's wrong?" he said, using a shocked tone and hugging her to his chest. "You can't be looking that gorgeous when I'm not there to protect you."

Nikki laughed, something she did a lot around him. She looped her arms around his neck, her eyes level with his smooth chin. "My feet aren't touching the ground so don't—"

His kiss cut her off. He took his time, angling his head and pressing his lips against hers, softly at first, then more firmly. She flexed her hips against his body and he stilled for a moment, then his tongue swept past her lips and swirled into her mouth. He tasted of wintergreen, and she was so, so glad she'd remembered to pop a mint herself.

"We should go inside," she whispered, dragging her mouth

away from his since he wouldn't stop kissing her. "No use giving the hands a show."

"Those guys are asleep."

"So, you have something against a nice soft queen-size bed and clean sheets?"

"I'm partial to kitchen counters myself." He'd switched to her neck, slowly planting moist kisses headed in the direction of her neckline.

She pushed her fingers through his hair, grabbing two handfuls and forcing his head back to see if he was serious. The teasing glint in his eyes earned him a yank.

"Ouch." He made a face. "I knew I should've gotten a haircut today."

"No, don't." She bit her lip. "Sorry. It's your hair. Do what you want."

"If you like it long, I'll keep it this way."

"Would you put me down? Please."

He swooped in for another quick kiss, then let her slide down his body. "Wait," he said. "Let's do that again."

Grinning, she took his hand and led him to the flagstone walkway. "We're going inside. Hey, I told you the front door was unlocked. Why did you wait out here?"

"I didn't feel right going in without you. Anyway, I wasn't waiting long and I used the time to return Aaron's call."

She'd wondered about whether they'd connected after she gave Trace the heads-up. "Were you able to have a civil conversation?"

"Oh, yeah. Aaron's okay. Just doing his job. I don't agree this time, that's all."

"Some of those guys tonight were getting awfully heated."

"Who? Eli and Lefty?"

She pushed open the door and pulled him inside. "Eli, Chip, Jerry, a few others I don't know by name. Even Sam put in his two cents."

Trace made sure they were locked in. "Two cents is about all that boy has to work with. He make you mad again tonight?"

"Sam is Sam. I'm trying not to react. Hey…" She giggled when he hooked an arm around her waist and hauled her up against him. Her body responded instantly, nipples beading, breaths coming quicker, dampness between her thighs….

"You smell good," he murmured, burying his face in the curve of her neck and shoulder.

"Oh, please, I smell like a bar. I'm taking a shower."

"Hmm, sounds like a good idea. I could use one, too." He plunged his fingers into her hair and gave her a light scalp massage.

She smiled because he smelled fresh and clean and a little like pine soap. "I didn't invite you," she said, letting her head loll back and her eyes close.

"I'm inviting myself."

"Trace, you are just—" She sighed and lifted her lashes. "You're amazing."

He stilled, aiming an expectant frown at her. "I'm waiting for the punch line."

"I hope you have all week." She brushed a kiss across his lips. "Do you have any idea how much admiration and respect the people here have for you?"

Surprise flickered in his face. He blinked, shaking his head and flushing. "Come on…" He lowered his arms and took her hand. "Let's go use up the hot water."

If she touched his cheeks she knew they'd be warm. He was embarrassed and she really should drop it, but she didn't understand why he'd prefer people to think he was a guy who got by on his looks and charm.

A sudden realization stunned her. No, it was her, that's what *she'd* thought. And so did the Sundance guests who chased him and flirted and made fools of themselves because all they saw was the sizzle but not the substance. The people who lived here, the ones who understood him, knew otherwise. To them, Trace was a man to be taken seriously.

"Okay, cowboy." She slipped her hand into his. "Show me what you got."

15

Trace soaped the back of her shoulders and watched the sudsy water sluice down her spine to the curve of her backside. Her skin looked as silky as it felt under his lips. She'd pulled her hair up into a messy knot, and he was trying his best not to get it wet, but sometimes he'd get distracted by the curve of her hip or the delicate slope of her neck.

"I think you already got that spot," she said, glancing back at him.

"You sure?"

"Yes, all three times."

He smiled and soaped the other side. "When you were going to community college, did anyone ask you to pose nude for art class?"

"What?" She laughed, and spun around to face him. "No."

"Fools." He circled the pad of his thumb over a taut pink nipple. "Though I can't deny I'm glad. I'd hate walking into a gallery and seeing you naked on a wall for everyone else to look at."

Nikki slid her palms up his chest, leaning into him, amusement dancing in her pretty dark eyes. "So, you go to art galleries often?"

"Nope."

"How many have you been to?"

He felt the right side of his mouth lifting. He ought to out-right lie. It would be harmless enough yet wipe that smug expression off her face. Skimming his hand along her hip, he waited until the right moment and said, "None," just as he slid his hand between her thighs.

She gasped and arched against his chest. "Sneaky."

The friction of her stiff nipples rubbing against him tested his willpower. "I forgot to soap down here." He parted her folds with the tips of his fingers, dipping inside only enough to make her tense.

"Pretty sure you didn't miss that spot, either," she whispered, ending with a soft moan that went straight to his cock.

"Better safe than horny."

She laughed and tugged at his chest hair.

"Isn't that the saying?" He braced his other hand against the tile wall for balance so he could better explore her. His fingers delved deeper, while he used his tongue to relearn the contours of her mouth.

She made the best damn sounds. Whimpers, moans, some of them a combination of both, others vibrating softly from her throat like a purr. She'd teased him about being quick on the draw, and he was a bit touchy about that because she wasn't wrong. What she didn't know was that it was all her fault. He hadn't had a problem like that since he was seventeen. She made him want her all the time, even when they were apart. If he so much as thought about the way her eyes flashed when she laughed, he wanted her. If he pictured her full pink lips parting right before they kissed, he wanted her. Hell, he could probably watch her fry an egg and want her right then and there.

Fortunately for him, he wasn't having a problem reloading quickly. What did worry him some was the degree of his infatuation. Something was off. He understood how watching her strip or kissing those lips could make him ache with a desperation that was humbling. But when they weren't even in the same room? Thinking about her still made him feel as if he was going to explode just as he had as a teenager. The difference now was that he cared about what was right for her instead of just his own satisfaction.

Maybe he needed to tell her this physical reaction wasn't normal for him. She might think he was lying, or maybe she'd be flattered that she reduced him to a helpless boy. That didn't sit well. Flattered was okay, but not the rest. Another alternative could be to wait it out…after they made love a few more times it was likely he'd settle down. Or hell, maybe he'd better start jerking off an hour before he planned on seeing her. They'd made love before they got into the shower, and while he was already hard again, he wasn't ready to pull the trigger.

He dragged his mouth from hers to find that sweet spot behind her ear. Her breathy moan came on cue, and he smiled against her skin.

"I think we've been in here long enough," she murmured, tilting her head back and almost getting her hair drenched.

"Okay, we'll get out." He put his arms around her waist and lifted her.

"What are you doing?" She clutched his shoulders. "I thought we were getting out."

"We will." He hefted her up a bit more, and she hooked a leg around his middle. "Put the other one up there, too."

With both of her legs wrapped around him, he kissed her right breast, then latched on to her taut nipple. He was careful using his teeth, not so much when he rolled and swirled his tongue over her tender skin. She pushed into his mouth every time she arched back and if she didn't stop, he was going to embarrass himself again.

With one hand cradling her firm backside, he kept her anchored to his waist, and used his other hand to tend that slick nub he knew would push her to the edge.

Her body tensed and she hid her face against the side of his neck, her short nails digging into his shoulder muscles.

"Kiss me, Nikki," he said, holding on to her ass when she started to squirm, and rubbing her faster.

She brought her head up, and looked at him, her eyes dazed. "I like that," she whispered sweetly, a little shyly.

"This?" He kept rubbing her, keeping the pressure and pace steady, though tightening his hold.

She nodded, and pressed her mouth to his, letting him coax her lips apart. He waited for her tongue to enter and touch his, then sweep inside. That's as far as she made it before she started whimpering, panting, teasing him with that soft purr. And puffing quick hot breaths into his mouth while she came.

NIKKI DRIED OFF his back, lingering on his ass, smiling when he flexed the muscles there. Her legs still weren't all that steady. She wouldn't totally relax until they were horizontal.

And had condoms within reach. That's what was scary about getting tuned up in the shower. She'd had to really slam on the brakes. At one point she'd barely been able to think beyond wanting him inside her.

"Okay, I'm dry enough," Trace said, turning to face her, and cupping her breasts. "And I'd prefer to keep a layer of skin, if you don't mind."

"And if I do?"

"I'll have to convince you otherwise." He leaned over, forcing her head back, knowing she wanted to make him break eye contact first. "I like that you're short."

"Why?"

"Want me to show you?"

"No." She pulled away and scrambled to the bedroom, wishing she'd thought to turn back the quilt and sheets.

"What did you think I was gonna do?" he asked with that mischievous smile that usually meant she was in for a treat.

She pointed to the other side of the bed before he touched her and made her forget what she was about to do. "You get over there and help me with the quilt."

"Yes, ma'am." He yanked his side back, ignoring her attempt at neatness. He caught her frown and said, "You know we're just gonna mess it up again."

"True." She laughed, happy, really happy, almost scary happy. Scary because the last time she'd felt this same light-headed giddiness had been with Luis. The high had only lasted a few days and involved too much tequila. It hadn't ended well.

Thinking of Luis reminded her of the last phone call to her mom. Shockingly, he'd shown up at her mother's apartment looking for Nikki. She hadn't seen or talked to him in over a year. Although Nikki harbored no hard feelings toward him, she had nothing to say to him, either. She hated that her mom had to run interference, but it was a relief that he found out Nikki had left Houston. Luis was another shameful part of her past she'd worked on forgetting.

"Nikki?"

She blinked, saw that Trace had already crawled into bed and was staring at her.

"You okay?"

"Where are the condoms?"

"Right here." He held up a handful of packets that he'd left on the nightstand.

"So optimistic." Grinning, she slid in beside him.

"What I lack in stamina, I make up for in frequency," he said, and they both laughed, although he flushed a bit. "Just so you know…that crack you made about me jumping the gun…that little problem I've been having is totally your fault."

"How?" She snuggled up to his chest, his arms around her.

keeping her warm and making her feel safe. Even knowing it wasn't forever, being with Trace still felt perfect.

"Other than being sexy as hell, I'm not sure. All I'm saying is this isn't the norm and I'm hoping it's temporary." He removed the clip holding up her hair and tossed it on the nightstand. "See?" he said, finger-combing the long strands that fell all over the place. "Just touching your hair, I'm getting hard again."

She checked to see if he was teasing because it didn't sound like it, and he really was semi-aroused.

Their gazes met. "And those eyes." His voice lowered and the tender smile he gave her nearly melted her heart. "Those beautiful brown eyes. I have no defense." He brushed the hair away from her face and kissed the side of her mouth. "And these lips…" He pressed a soft kiss at the other corner. "It's a wonder I can keep my mind on anything else."

A wave of shyness swept her. "You're such a player," she said, giving him a light tap on his chest. Regret was instant.

She saw the hurt in his eyes.

"I can't blame you for thinking I'm no better than a tomcat. But those women out at the Sundance, they don't mean anything— No. Wait a minute." He frowned. "Have you ever seen me seriously flirt with one of the guests?"

"You've got to be kidding."

"I'm talking about since you've come back. No kidding now, at the Sundance or at the Watering Hole, can you name one time that I flirted?"

Nikki got up on her elbow and leaned back to get a good look at his face. "You flirt all the time, though I'm not saying you shouldn't. It's your business."

"Now you think about this," he said, no teasing in his gaze at all. "I usually respond when they flirt, at least I try to be pleasant. Sometimes they're annoying as hell and it's all I can do to make myself smile."

"Trace, stop. You don't owe me an explanation." Laying her cheek back on his chest, she ran her hand down his belly. "We have more important things to do."

"This is important to me," he said quietly, covering her hand and bringing it to a halt. "It's only you, Nikki. I'm not seeing anyone else." He kissed her hair. "I don't want anyone else."

She didn't even know how to respond to that, or to the flutters he'd set off. Was she supposed to say it back? Thank him? Briefly she considered asking him to be more specific, then discarded the idea. "Okay," she finally mumbled when it appeared he wasn't going to help her out.

He sighed, released her hand and cupped the back of her head. "So where were we?"

Good. This part she knew how to handle. She brushed her lips across his right pec, started to work her way lower, but he slid down, startling her with an openmouthed kiss that left her without air. His tongue demanded entry, then made a thorough sweep she could feel all the way to her core.

It wasn't just his kiss that sent her reeling. Every touch made her hyperaware that it was Trace's hand, Trace's fingers. Each gasp was filled with more than lust. He wanted only her. This good man, the one she'd dismissed so flippantly. No wonder she didn't know how to handle the pure want in his gaze.

She spread her legs, needing him closer. The way his eyebrows rose as his pupils dilated made her flush even more than his intimate caress.

When he was settled, resting on his elbows, his body blanketing her own, he smiled. "I'm not guaranteeing a thing," he said. "You drive me crazy, you know that? Straight out of my mind. And when I'm in you, no matter how I try, I can't seem to control myself."

She brushed her fingers across his cheekbone, then curved

her hand to the back of his neck. "Just the way I like you. Out of control."

His eyes staying on her face, Trace turned to kiss her arm. "I know something else you might like."

"Oh?"

He slid down further, and she could feel the whisper of moist breath on the skin between her ribs, the pressure of his warm lips just below her navel. She sucked in a breath, waiting, trying to watch, but she could only see the top of his head.

The first glide of his tongue sent a jolt through her. She automatically bucked, and he held on to her hips, keeping her still, and using his tongue to drive every last thought from her head until she completely shattered.

NIKKI HEARD THE COLLIES barking and glanced out her bedroom window. She didn't recognize the blue Cadillac bumping along the gravel driveway, but then she hadn't expected to. It was two minutes to four. The attorney was right on time. If only a flat had delayed him long enough for her to leave for work. Though she supposed that wish was a little unkind.

The man was only here to do his job, and she'd promised Matt she'd behave. Sitting quietly and listening wouldn't kill her. It didn't mean she had to agree or accept anything from Wallace. She still hadn't gotten over the shock that he'd named her in his will at all. However, both she and Matt were offended on Lucy's behalf. Loyal to a fault and she hadn't even gotten a mention. They knew because Matt had asked Frank Kessler if Lucy should also be present.

After checking her hair in the mirror so she could leave for the Watering Hole as soon as they were done, she stopped at her bed. She'd made it up, something she did about every other day, but this morning she'd left out Trace's pillow. Picking it up, she lifted it to her nose. She could still smell him. Some of the dread drained from her. If the attorney made her edgy, she'd daydream about Trace, she decided, or replay last night.

Oh, God, that could get her in trouble. Maybe it was better she wasn't all starry-eyed. Or thinking about Trace at the moment. If she was in too good a mood, no telling what she might agree to.

She hurried down the stairs and headed toward the voices coming from the den. Sitting on the red leather couch, papers spread on the coffee table in front of him, Frank Kessler looked out of place. He wore a sharp navy blue suit, yellow tie and shiny black shoes, his gray hair slicked back. She would've guessed he was from New York, not Billings, Montana.

He rose as soon as he saw her and extended his hand. "Nikita Flores," he said, "it's a pleasure to meet you. Frank Kessler."

"Um, I go by Nikki." She didn't care for his weak handshake or the intense curiosity in his small dark eyes.

Matt had already claimed the chair that matched the couch, so she perched on the edge of the floral-patterned chaise close to the stone fireplace.

Mr. Kessler smiled and gestured to the unoccupied side of the couch. "I promise I won't bite."

She returned the smile. "I might." Then darted a grudging glance at Matt. He wasn't amused. "Just kidding," she said to Mr. Kessler, who appeared unfazed. "I'm fine here."

"First off," he said, "please accept my condolences on the loss of your father."

A snide remark nearly tripped off her tongue, but she drew in a breath, reminding herself the goal was to get this reading over with. "Thank you."

"Matt has requested that we keep this short because you have to go to work." He'd slipped on a pair of glasses and was sifting through several legal-size papers while he spoke.

"The Gunderson Trust is quite straightforward. The land and house, including any and all structures, are covered by the trust. Paternity hasn't been challenged, and since Wallace legally acknowledged you as his daughter, Nikki, in the eyes of the law—"

"When?"

Kessler looked at her over the rim of his glasses. "The beginning of March…I believe it was a couple of weeks after you and Matt had visited him. He signed an affidavit verifying your relationship to him, and then he updated his will."

She wasn't sure why she'd bothered to ask. What did it matter? Wallace had always known she existed. Legally recognizing her didn't make a damn bit of difference. "Sorry. I shouldn't have interrupted."

"Ask anything you want, Nikki," Matt said, and she noticed his expression seemed strained. "Now's your chance."

"I'm good for now," she said.

"Feel free to stop me at any time." Kessler seemed patient and professional, but something about him bugged her. "Let's see," he said, his attention going back to the document. "In accordance with the terms of the trust, the land and structures, as I mentioned, now belong equally to the two of you. What gets tricky and isn't clear is ownership of the livestock, which is worth a substantial sum and we'll get to that in a minute.

"Equipment, inventory, vehicles registered to the Lone Wolf, those sorts of things obviously aren't covered by the trust, which was drawn nearly a hundred years ago. Those items are considered personal property and Wallace has left them to Matt. I have an itemized list for each of you. Any questions so far?" He looked up until they both shook their heads.

No point arguing now. Nikki knew division of the land and house was something she and Matt had to sort out in private, which should be a short conversation, given she wanted nothing. But knowing Matt, it wasn't a discussion she was looking forward to. He'd been okay earlier, but now he seemed irritable. She hoped it wasn't over Wallace leaving him all that stuff and not including her. She didn't give a crap about any of it.

"Now, about the livestock." Kessler's gaze moved over the words on the next document. "Fortunately you two are on good terms, that makes things easier," he murmured, half to himself. "That's not always the case…"

Nikki yawned, tuning out Kessler and wishing she'd made coffee. After Trace had left at eight-thirty she'd gone back to sleep. And still she'd only managed to get a total of five hours. Poor Trace had to go move cattle to another pasture, though he'd promised to grab a nap before meeting her at the bar later.

Last night had been sheer heaven. He knew exactly how to touch her, knew where she was the most sensitive and above all, he'd shown her a tenderness she hadn't known existed. Normally she didn't like waking up with a guy. She wanted them gone long before it was time to jump in the shower. But everything was upside down when it came to Trace. Several times today she'd found herself plotting ways to get him to stay over tonight.

"Nikki?"

At the sound of Matt's voice, she straightened. Both he and Kessler were staring at her, and she had a feeling she'd missed quite a bit. "Sorry, what was that?"

"You might want to listen to this," Matt said, his expression more relaxed.

Kessler read directly from the will. "'To my daughter, Nikita Flores, I bequeath the balance of my cash holdings at the time of my death.'" The attorney switched his gaze to a ledger sheet. "As of this morning, including interest, that amount is $172,548."

Nikki blinked. "I don't understand."

Matt smiled, leaning forward, his elbows resting on his thighs. "That money is yours, Nik. Wallace left it to you."

She would've thought she heard wrong if Matt hadn't looked so pleased. This was crazy. She really didn't want anything from the man, but this was huge. That kind of money could change her life. Truly give her a fresh start.

"However, there is a stipulation." Kessler's face went blank and he focused solely on Nikki. "You only get the money if you sign your share of the Lone Wolf over to Matt."

She felt as if someone had punched her in the stomach.

"Bullshit." Matt glared at the older man. "Nobody can mess with the trust. I know that for a fact."

"You're right," Mr. Kessler said calmly. "Nikki couldn't sell her half to anyone, but she can waive her claim and sign it over to you because you're a Gunderson."

"So is Nikki."

"No one's disputing that, Matthew." Kessler removed his glasses and rubbed the bridge of his nose. "Wallace wanted you to have the Lone Wolf. That's all. I will say this, I personally think this is his way of making it up to you for past wrongs."

Matt's anger radiated from across the room. "Screw him. The money is yours, Nikki. You're not signing over any rights."

"I'm afraid that's not up to you." Mr. Kessler sighed. "Look, keep this simple. Legally, you'll need to sign the waiver in order to release the money. After that you're free to do what you want. Do you understand?"

Numb, except for the ache in her chest, Nikki got his meaning. But she didn't care about the Lone Wolf. Right now she didn't even care about the money. Wallace was trying to buy her off, and that hurt more than she thought possible. He'd been a sick old man on his deathbed, and yet somehow he managed to get in that extra slap in the face even after death.

She had to give it to him. It took effort to be that much of a bastard.

Matt was saying something to the attorney, maybe even to her, but she hadn't been listening. "I'll need time to think it over," she said, cutting Matt off and getting to her feet. "Is that all?"

Kessler frowned. "Well, no, there's more."

"Do you need me?"

The older man slowly shook his head. "I guess not."

"Nikki, wait." Matt looked heartsick.

"I'm fine." She forced a smile. This wasn't his fault. She didn't want him to feel bad. Wallace had been a jerk until the end. It shouldn't have been a surprise, and it sure as hell shouldn't make a difference. A sob broke in her throat, and she hurried to the door.

16

NIKKI HEARD A NOISE, turned her head and saw Trace, but not Gypsy. "What are you doing here?" She dabbed at her cheeks to make sure they weren't damp before he got too close. She hadn't cried really, just got a little teary. "Were we supposed to meet today?" she asked, so confused she couldn't think straight.

"No." He jerked a thumb over his shoulder. "I have my truck. Guess you didn't hear me drive up."

"I thought you were moving cattle." She slid off the rock she'd been sitting on for the past hour and dusted off her butt while she waited for him to reach her.

"I was." He left the trail, cut through the tall grass and put his arms around her. "Rough day, huh?"

"Is that a shot in the dark or did you talk to Matt?"

"He called."

Nikki sighed. Pressing her cheek against his chest, taking comfort in the strong steady beat of his heart, she felt some of the tension leave her body. "He shouldn't have done that."

"Of course he should have. If it were Rachel, I'd have done the same for him."

Matt and Rachel were getting married in a few months so

it wasn't at all the same. But Nikki appreciated the sentiment
"He didn't know I was here, though."

"He said you were upset…" Trace brushed a kiss on her
forehead. "I figured you might come here." He sighed. "Wal
lace always was a bastard. That didn't change. I know it's
hard, but don't let it get to you."

"Wow, Matt told you everything."

He leaned back and studied her face, touching the outside
corner of her eye with his thumb. "You mind?"

She blinked, hoping there were no tears ready to fall. "
would've told you myself…eventually. It's not about the Lone
Wolf or the money."

"I know that." He sat on the huge rock she'd used as a
bench and pulled her onto his lap.

Nikki started to object…but it felt nice being cocooned by
his chest and arms. "I hate that you left work. I'm really okay."

"You think I could do anything but come find you?" He
stroked her back, rubbed her arm. "Remember that thing
about you not being alone anymore?"

Dammit. So much for no more tears. Sometimes kindness
was the worst…

"Hey." He ignored her efforts to hide her face and caught
her chin. "Did I just do that?" He looked into her watery
eyes, the alarm in his expression restoring some of her calm

"Yes, you're being too nice. Stop it."

"Sorry. I can't do that." He touched his lips to hers, the
gentle kiss meant only to soothe.

"How did Matt sound? Is he okay?"

"He was worried. I called him as soon as I spotted your
truck and he seemed relieved. Didn't tell him where you were
No need to give up our favorite make-out spot."

Nikki smiled. "He was so angry, even with the attorney
who was only doing his job." She watched a squirrel scurrying

up a tree with something in its mouth. "Now that I've had time to think, for Matt's sake, I'm glad Wallace did what he did."

"You might want to fill me in more," Trace said, frowning as if he couldn't see her point. "Matt gave me the gist but he was pissed and not too clear."

She wasn't thrilled to recap the meeting, but it was a good test to see if she truly was making peace with Wallace. "You know about the Gunderson Trust," she said, and he nodded so she skipped that part, summed up the rest, digging for composure when she got to the one provision in the will. "The money he left, it's a lot, around $172,000." Trace's brows shot up. Apparently Matt hadn't told him how much. "Basically he wants me gone, even though he's dead. I get the cash if I sign over my rights to Matt."

Trace didn't look surprised, only furious. "I know…what I don't get is why you're okay with Wallace being a manipulative jackass or how you can believe that helps Matt."

"At first I was mad and hurt that he thought he had to protect his precious family land from me. After all, I'm not a 'true' Gunderson, only his bastard." She shook her head when Trace started to object, and regretted her bitter tone. Clearly she had more work to do on herself. "But the attorney said something that made me think. I'm not sure that stipulation had much to do with me. Wallace might've been trying to make amends to Matt. He wouldn't care about the money, not with what he's stashed from his winnings. But Matt loves the Lone Wolf."

"Nice thought, except there's no way Matt would be satisfied with you being cut out. He probably hates Wallace even more now."

She sighed, understanding the logic. She herself despised Wallace more for what he'd done to Matt than for abandoning her. "After the hurt and anger dies down, I'll talk to him. Wallace was screwed up. But I want Matt to believe that his father had tried to make things up to him the only way he knew how."

His brows puckered, Trace studied her with no less concern. "You're taking this a whole lot better than I imagined."

"You should've seen me an hour ago. I thought, wow, Wallace was scum and *he* thought I wasn't good enough to be a part of his family."

"Jesus, Nikki." Letting out a harsh breath, he forced her to look at him. "Don't ever go there. You're amazing."

She couldn't help but smile. "And you're…" She touched his stubbled jaw. "I was so wrong about you."

He gave her a crooked grin. "You figured I was just another pretty face, and hollow inside like a chocolate Easter bunny."

"Actually, yes." She laughed. "Not the chocolate bunny, that part didn't occur to me."

Trace hugged her, his quiet growl the sound of pure contentment. "That's a lot of money you're about to get. More than enough to go back to school if you want. They have a few good colleges in Kalispell. Not that I'm being selfish."

Nikki stiffened. "I haven't decided if I'm going to accept the money."

"Why wouldn't you?"

"I never wanted anything from him. You know that."

"Hell, Wallace isn't here. You'd only be hurting yourself by turning it down."

She slipped off his lap. "I'd know the money came from him."

Trace caught her hand. "Don't be hasty. You need time. And don't forget about school," he said while doing light circles on her wrist with his thumb. "Is your hesitation about the Lone Wolf? You know Matt would never let you give up your share."

"I don't want the Lone Wolf, either. I don't even know if I'm cut out for this slow country life." She hadn't meant to raise her voice or be quite so honest, but it shocked her to see the raw disappointment in his eyes.

"Maybe not," he said grimly, tugging her close again. "But if you don't take the money and just disappear, Wallace wins." Trace put his hands on her waist. "You're still emotional, and you and Matt have a lot to discuss. Promise me you'll take your time to decide."

She nodded, not sure if he'd pulled her toward him or if she'd stepped forward. He cradled her between his spread thighs, his arms wrapping around her and hers circling his neck. Their foreheads touching, neither of them moved. He was right. She was still emotional. For the better part of an hour, she'd thought about the past, from the mess with Garrett and the prom to how she'd foolishly tried to find comfort in Luis. Worst of all was how often she'd hurt her mother.

She didn't want to do that to Trace, too. He was so amazing in many, many ways, and much more than someone like her deserved. Wallace had been a bastard, all right. But who was to say he was wrong? Maybe she really wasn't good enough. Maybe she never would be.

TRACE MISSED OBLITERATING his thumb by a hair. He threw the hammer down and cursed his stupidity. "That's it. I'm done for the day. You quit, too, if you want," he said to Josh. "These warped boards will still be here tomorrow."

Tempted as he was to leave the tools scattered, Trace crouched down and started throwing everything into the toolbox. The way they landed all helter-skelter, he'd never be able to close the damn thing.

"I'll do that," Josh said. "Go."

"Nah, that's all right." He'd feel guilty as hell leaving his friend with the mess. Bad enough Trace had been moody since seeing Nikki, no need to let Josh take the brunt of it.

"I'm not trying to be nice." Josh collected the rags. "It's self-defense. Get out of here before I end up on crutches."

A grudging smile tugged at Trace's mouth. "I haven't been that bad."

Josh gave him a long look. "You almost ran over my toes with the four-wheeler. And I'm pretty sure you've used every cussword you know in English and Spanish."

Trace gave up on closing the toolbox. "Not all of them."

Josh took it from him. "You going to the Watering Hole after supper? I'll buy you a beer."

That was part of Trace's problem. He couldn't decide if it was better to go see her or stay away. What he really wanted to do was talk to Matt about her, but he knew that would only lead to trouble—if Nikki went behind his back and discussed him with Rachel, he'd sure be pissed.

"Yeah, I'll go. But I'm buying. I reckon that's the least I can do." He watched Josh patiently rearrange the tools and close the box. "When do you leave to see your girl?"

"Not for three weeks. Fourth of July weekend." Josh's grin was wider than the Grand Canyon. "Can't come fast enough."

"You going all the way to New York?"

"Nope. Haley's meeting me partway."

"Where?"

Josh's grin faded. "Why?"

Trace shrugged. "Just curious." It was more than that. Haley had been a Sundance guest when Josh met her. She lived in Manhattan, and Trace had wondered how that would pan out for them. Josh had never doubted they could make it work, but Trace had. He hoped he wouldn't be put to the same long-distance test with Nikki. "Come on, where are you guys meeting?"

Josh sighed. "Disneyland."

"What?"

"You heard right."

They were heading out of the barn but Trace stopped and laughed. "You haven't seen Haley in how many months, and you're taking her to Disneyland? Son, you need your head screwed on tighter."

"It's not me." He held up his hands. "Haley wants to go there. I didn't argue." Josh narrowed his eyes. "If Nikki wanted to go to Siberia, tell me you wouldn't be packed in two minutes."

"Shut up." Trace started walking again, veering off toward the house.

"You wanna ride with me to town?" Josh called after him.

"No, I'm taking my truck."

"Right." Josh's laugh grated on his nerves. "In case you-know-who wants to go to Siberia."

Trace flipped him off without a look back. A guest could've seen him, but so what. His mood wasn't getting any better, and he figured he ought to skip dinner. Sitting at the table and trying to be nice would be torture. He wasn't even hungry. And he sure as hell didn't want to make small talk.

What a fool he'd been to think Nikki could be happy living here. She'd get bored sooner or later. Bored with Blackfoot Falls, bored with him. It wasn't so much what she'd said about not being cut out for the country, it was how she'd said it. He had a bad feeling she'd already made up her mind.

It still appalled him to think he'd actually been tempted to discourage her from taking the money. If she was broke, she'd have to stay. But with all that cash, she could set herself up someplace real nice. Man, he couldn't stand to think about her leaving. He had no right to ask her to stay, he knew that, but if the time came, he just might beg her.

That would be something. He never imagined he'd have to humble himself for a woman. Not that he thought he was too good for a little humility. Finding a willing woman had always been easy for him. The guys used to tease him about being able to pick and choose. It had been all in good fun, but it also had been the truth. He didn't like this new game plan.

He stopped in the mudroom to scrape his boots. They were in terrible shape but not so bad they'd harm the wood floors. Rachel would yell if she saw him sneaking in with them on, but he didn't care. Besides, he thought he'd heard her on the porch with the guests. It was beer and margarita time for them. And the perfect opportunity for him to creep upstairs unnoticed.

He opened the door to the kitchen and she stood right there in front of him, dropping a can into the recycle bin.

Her gaze went straight to his boots, eyes narrowing to a glare. "What are you doing?"

"I don't want to hear it," he said, putting up a warning finger. Hilda stood at the stove, and she turned in surprise at his rough tone. "Trust me. Bad time to get into it with me," he added to make sure Rachel backed off.

"I know," she said softly. "I really hate Wallace. I do."

"Have you seen Matt?"

She shook her head. "We talked on the phone. I'll see him later. How's Nikki?"

"I know she went to work." He rubbed the tension tightening the back of his neck. "Count me out for dinner."

"Can I at least make you a sandwich?"

"No, thanks. I'm going to town…" He sighed. Hell, everyone knew about him and Nikki at this point. "To the bar. If I get hungry I'll grab something at Marge's."

Rachel nodded. "Go. I'll see you later." She blinked, then her eyes rounded with surprise. "Maybe at the Lone Wolf," she said, laughing and blushing. "Oh, God."

"Ah." He got it. If he spent the night with Nikki it would be kind of weird knowing his kid sister was down the hall with Matt. Trace just laughed. "We bump into each other in the dark and I'll pretend I don't know you."

"Same here." She bit her lip and glanced at Hilda, who kept turning over pieces of sizzling fried chicken, while paying them no attention. Though she must've heard.

Rachel abruptly turned away, trying not to laugh, and he raced out of the kitchen and up the stairs to his room in record time. He lingered in the shower, letting the warm spray hit the back of his neck and stiff shoulders. He had to stop giving his thoughts free rein. Whether Nikki stayed or left, him worrying about it wouldn't change a damn thing.

Ten minutes later, the idea that she could pack up and leave at any time still rattled him no matter what he told himself. With Wallace gone, and Matt busy with setting a new course for the Lone Wolf, there wouldn't be much to keep Nikki around here. Trace wanted to think she'd stay for him, but he hadn't come out and asked her to, or told her how he felt about her. Of course he still hadn't quite narrowed that down yet.

He dried himself off, pulled on clean jeans and took a brown Western-cut shirt out of his closet. The guys would razz him again for wearing his good clothes, and he was in just the right mood to tell them where to shove it.

The ride to town went by quickly. Already there was no street parking in front of the Watering Hole. He saw Nikki's pickup next to the bank and grabbed a spot two trucks away.

Music spilled out onto the sidewalk. The heavy wood door was no match when someone cranked up the jukebox. He would've liked it a whole lot better if the bar wasn't so crowded, but nothing to do about it. He'd barely made it inside when someone whistled, then he heard a catcall and laughter. It was the shirt. Screw them.

Nikki stood at the end of the bar where she turned in her drink orders, looking over her shoulder to see what the noise was about. She saw him and smiled.

He actually felt a strange sensation in his chest. Man, it was going to be hard to walk over and not kiss her. But she looked relaxed as if this was any other night, and for now that was good enough. She moved over to make room for him, and he didn't hesitate.

"This is early for you," she said once he crowded in between her and a young cowboy sitting on a stool.

"I skipped supper." He almost touched her cheek, but diverted his hand to plow through his hair at the last second. "Everyone else seems to have had the same idea."

"It's been crazy busy since Sadie unlocked the door." Her gaze moved over his shirt. "You look nice. Smell nice, too," she whispered, swaying against him, her lids at half-mast.

"Don't go starting anything we can't finish," he muttered, afraid his cock mistook that as an invitation to party.

"Oh, right. Sorry."

"Trace?" Sadie was a bit farther down the bar, mixing a drink. "Beer?"

"Don't worry about me. I can wait."

"Oh, shoot, I was about to help fill mugs." Nikki scribbled something on her pad, then swung to the other side of the bar.

He waited until she had a pitcher and mugs lined up. "Before I forget, we should set a time for a riding lesson tomorrow."

"Oh." She fiddled with the tap. Once the beer began flowing, she nodded. "Good idea. I'd prefer the afternoon if that's okay."

Relief surged through his body. In the few seconds it took for her to agree, he'd realized how much he needed to hear she didn't plan on going anywhere…at least not tomorrow. "Just let me know when and I'll be at our spot."

With a fretful frown, she met his eyes. "About later," she said softly, her voice tinged with disappointment. "It sounds as if you're not coming over tonight."

One more rush of relief and he was going to need to sit down. "I haven't been invited yet."

Nikki's smile lit up every dark cloud hanging over his heart. "Silly boy, I want you every night."

The relief that flowed through him nearly knocked him sideways. He might not be certain about where he and Nikki were headed, but the idea that he wouldn't have the chance to find out had been killing him.

She wasn't leaving tonight. Tomorrow things would seem better. And after that…he had no idea, but at least time no longer felt like a fight he couldn't win.

17

Nikki was starting to get cold feet. Every time the door opened, dread kicked up another notch and she couldn't be sorrier she'd made that deal with Karina. So much had changed between Nikki and Trace since the night she'd thought Karina was trying to pick him up. He wouldn't think the woman's real proposal was funny, and now neither did Nikki. Oh, he might've been a good sport had Karina approached him at the Sundance or in private. But here at the Watering Hole in front of Sam and the others, he wouldn't be amused.

In the three days since the will had been read, Nikki still hadn't completely made up her mind about whether to accept Wallace's money but it no longer ate at her. The more time she spent with Trace, the more she saw the appeal of sticking around, at least until she figured out for sure what she wanted to do with the rest of her life.

Truthfully, the thought of leaving him behind was hard to contemplate. At least for now, when things felt so right. She'd been enjoying her hot nights and jam-packed days with him too much. He'd even coaxed her on top of Gypsy for ten whole minutes yesterday.

While she had time between customers, she washed mugs,

ordering herself not to check the clock. Again. When her mind occasionally drifted to the decision she had to make, she always seemed to hear Trace's voice telling her not to let Wallace win. Matt's solution was for her to sign over her share, accept the money and then he'd reverse the process the very next day.

It took a few seconds to realize her phone had buzzed. It was Trace. She saw that Karina was busy studying the jukebox, and Nikki motioned to let Sadie know she had to step outside for a minute. She answered on her way to the door. It opened and Trace entered, grinning, his cell phone pressed to his ear.

"I miss you," he said, to which she responded with a groan and "You big dope."

His laugh drew Karina's attention. Great. Too late for Nikki to drag him outside. She sighed and nodded at an older cowboy signaling for a pitcher refill.

Trace followed her to the bar and grabbed a stool while she slipped around to the other side. "Come on." Staring at her, his grin faltered. "You can't be mad."

"No, but you might be." While filling the pitcher, she looked past him and watched Karina close in.

"Why?" He started to turn his head, caught a glimpse of Karina and snapped back to face the bar.

"I leave tomorrow, cowboy." Karina slid onto the empty stool beside him. "Last chance for me to buy you a drink."

"No, thanks. Just came by to visit Nikki."

Karina smiled at her. "You know how to make an appletini or should I wait for Sadie?"

"I can manage," she said.

Karina waited until Nikki started on her appletini, then turned to Trace. "I have a business proposition for you."

He lifted a brow. "A what?"

"A business proposition. This has been a working vacation for me. A scouting trip." Karina reached into the neckline of her low-cut blouse and brought out a business card. She passed it to Trace.

He seemed reluctant to accept it. Finally he did, then frowned at the writing. "Okay," he said, drawing out the word.

"My company is staging a campaign to find a cowboy to be the face of our latest line of fragrances."

"Why are you telling me?" Trace narrowed his gaze on Karina, but not before glancing around.

"I think you'd have a great shot at it. We're doing something fun and different to engage consumers in the selection process. We're streamlining the list of candidates by making a calendar and—"

"Hold on right there." He lowered his voice and slid a quick look to his left, then at the door when it creaked open. "I'm not interested," he said quietly, putting down her card by her drink.

Nikki's breath caught. He looked so embarrassed and she hated, hated that she'd played any part in this. How could she have thought this was funny? A week ago she'd barely known him. Not the real Trace. She'd stubbornly clung to a stereotype she'd adopted the first night she'd met him in February. It was different now. She knew better, but he was going to be mad and she couldn't blame him.

Karina started in again, trying to convince him with flattery and large sums of money. Trace, without being rude, tried his best to get her to tone it down. The few folks sitting at nearby tables had turned toward them, their curiosity piqued. Even Sadie had moved closer.

Nikki cleared her throat. "Karina, it's not going to happen. You'll have to find someone else."

The woman swung her a disappointed frown. "You were supposed to help convince him. Thanks for nothing."

Trace stared at Nikki. His expression of disbelief branded her a traitor.

"I need to explain," she said.

"You sure do." He surprised her with a short laugh. "A calendar?"

"Yes." Karina clearly misread his reaction and jumped back in. "You'd be perfect as Mr. March."

Trace shook his head, his lips pressed thin. "She's right. Not gonna happen."

The woman sighed, but seemed otherwise unfazed. She took a final sip of her drink, reached into her cleavage again, then laid a ten on the bar. "Keep my card in case you change your mind. I may come back through Montana next month." She got off the stool, paused to tilt her head and study him a moment. "Maybe Mr. July. Tight button-fly jeans, no shirt, behind you a spray of fireworks against the night sky."

Nikki pressed her own lips together to keep from laughing at the look of astonishment on Trace's face. It really wasn't funny, and she was so lucky he didn't seem furious with her.

"Think about it." Karina shrugged, gave him a saucy wink and walked off.

"Mr. July," Trace muttered. "Shit."

A hand from the Lone Wolf called out, "Oh, Mr. July," in a high-pitched voice and earned a glare from Nikki that shut him right up. The laughter that followed was predictable, but Trace ignored it all.

"So you were in cahoots with her," he said, and there was a hint of hurt in his eyes. "That's surprising."

"Oh. No. It's not like that." Nikki took a deep breath. "When she explained why she was here, I thought it was funny and asked to be there when she told you. I barely knew you then." She leaned on the bar and almost took his hand before she stopped herself. "I forgot all about it until today. I was going to warn you. That's why I left a message."

"I guess I blew that part." He moved his hand closer to hers. They weren't touching, but they might as well have been.

"Thanks for not being mad," she said, still amazed he hadn't even raised his voice. "Even though you had every right."

"I'm a pretty laid-back guy. Usually willing to hear someone out." Smiling, he leaned closer. "Or let her make it up to me."

Nikki let out a loud laugh that drew more than a few looks. She didn't care, and it seemed that neither did Trace. But then she noticed a customer waving his empty mug at her and she straightened with a sigh. "I have to get back to work."

"Well that sucks." Trace let his gaze slide down her body as though he had much better plans for her.

"Stop it right now, McAllister," she warned, and picked up her tray as she came around the bar.

The door creaked open as it had a dozen times in the past hour. Normally she ignored it unless she was expecting Trace. She didn't know what made her look now, but she turned, and felt the blood drain from her face.

Luis.

How? He was supposed to be in Houston. It wasn't possible that he could be here. Her mother promised she hadn't told him where Nikki was living.

His dark hair was shorter and he wore nice jeans, not his usual baggy ones. The blue knit shirt was not his style, and didn't hide the tattoo sleeve that crawled from his wrist up the side of his neck. He couldn't have looked more out of place.

Her feet felt like lead weights. She couldn't seem to move, only watch his gaze pan the room and wait for him to get to her. Her tray was still loaded and she needed to set it down or risk spilling everything.

Luis finally spotted her. She found no relief in the faint curve of his mouth. A smile could go either way with him.

He could be cruel when he was using. Nikki didn't care that he'd sworn to her mom he'd been clean for a year.

It finally registered that the room had grown quiet except for the country music coming from the jukebox. She had to do something. She glanced at the tables closest to her, then set the tray down on the one that had space. Everyone could sort out their own drinks.

She saw him start for the bar and hurried to intercept him, wiping her clammy palms on her jeans. She was able to head him off. But only because he stopped when he saw her coming.

"Hi." She tried to swallow around the lump of panic lodged in her throat. "What are you doing here?"

"Hello, Nikita." Luis moved to kiss her, but she sidestepped him before realizing he'd only been going for her cheek. His touch on her arm was light, then fell away. This wasn't the same man she remembered. "I understand," he said quietly, giving her room.

Obviously unaware of the drama, someone from the back yelled for their beer. Nikki automatically turned and caught Trace's eye. She gave him a small shake of her head and hoped he stayed put. "I'm working," she told Luis while subtly walking him toward the door. "I really can't talk." She saw Sadie retrieve the tray and carry it to the back.

Of course everyone in the bar stared at them.

"No hurry. I don't drink any more but I can have a soda while I wait," Luis said, studying her face. "You look good."

"You shouldn't be here."

"I had to come. I got myself clean. Just like I promised you I would." He sounded more urgent. "I want you back. You said you'd give me another chance if I turned my life around."

"Luis, I was a kid when I said that." She could barely remember the promise she'd made in another life. "I've changed, too."

"I have savings now. Not drug money. I work at my cousin's body shop. Totally legit. A few years and I can buy it from him." He touched her cheek. "Everything I've done is for you, baby."

She pushed his hand away. "I'm not going back to Houston."

"Then we'll go someplace else. Start fresh."

"No, Luis. I wish you hadn't come." She'd always hated the loud country music from the jukebox. Where was it now when she needed it? "Please just leave."

Luis looked past her, his shoulders squaring, and she knew it had to be Trace.

"Nikki, you all right?" he asked from just behind her.

"Fine." She turned and forced a smile for him. "It's okay."

Trace met her eyes. Her weak assurance hadn't been enough.

"You heard her." Luis stayed calm, at least for him, but some of the old belligerence bled into his voice. "Go back and drink your beer, cowboy. And mind your own goddamn business."

"See that's the thing." Trace gave him a thin smile. "Nikki *is* my business, and she doesn't want you here."

"Please stop." She held on to Trace's arm and put her other hand up to Luis. "Please, both of you."

Luis swore. "Tell me how my wife is your business."

Nikki couldn't breathe. Her chest tightened and her throat closed. She reeled at Trace's shocked expression, but it was nothing compared to the pain in his eyes.

Trace waited for her denial. This stranger with the tats had to be lying. So why wasn't she saying anything? She just stared, looking guiltier by the second. What the hell? "Nikki?"

She sucked in air, putting a hand to her throat, still staring at him, shame written all over her face. "It's not like that…"

She briefly hung her head, then looked at the other man. "Luis, just go. If you ever cared for me, you'll leave. Now."

Indecision flickered in his eyes. "I only came to get what's mine," he said, and stroked her arm.

Trace watched her delayed reaction in pulling away. "Sorry, dude," he said to the guy, anger and stunned humiliation digging their hooks deeper into him. "My mistake."

"Please, Trace." Her voice was so faint he almost hadn't heard her as he walked around them and out the door.

He got to the sidewalk, thought about stopping and bending over until his head cleared. The truck was still a block away. He pushed on.

Nikki was married? Jesus. That wasn't the kind of thing that could slip someone's mind. He hated to believe the guy, and he wouldn't have if only she'd spoken up. Even if she was legally separated, that would've been okay with him. Things might've gone differently for them until she was divorced, hell, he didn't know.

He jogged the last few yards to his truck, climbed inside with his heart pounding as if it would burst. Did Matt know she was married? Rachel?

It didn't matter because every time Nikki had kissed him, each time they'd made love, she'd lied to him. Not just words gave a lie teeth and she'd taken plenty of bites. What hurt worse was that they'd confided in each other. She'd confessed some pretty heavy stuff, so had he. To think he'd been humbled by her trust… How could he have missed it? He'd thought he knew her. More than any woman he'd ever met. The irony was, he'd finally made up his mind that tonight was the night. He was going to come right out and prove to her that he was in this thing one hundred percent.

He'd believed with everything he had that Nikki was not only brave and strong and independent, but honest down to the bone. It'd never once occurred to him that she could be hiding so much of herself. Not after all they'd been through.

He stuck the key in the ignition and started the truck. His gaze went back to the Watering Hole door. No one had left since him. She was still in there with that guy. Her husband.

As he pulled out of his spot, the fire inside him turned cold. He should have listened to his instincts. Realized he wasn't thinking straight. Twenty-seven was too young to go all in on a relationship. Maybe not for some guys, but for him? His gut had warned him, but that voice had been drowned out by his damn hormones.

He drove slow, careful. Everyone in the bar had just seen him get squashed like a bug. By tomorrow morning, he doubted there was anyone in town, hell, in the county who wouldn't have heard about how she'd made him look like a fool. Just thinking about facing Sam again made Trace's insides crawl.

Why hadn't she told him? Was it because she'd known all along she was going to go back to Luis? Did she love the guy? Is that why she'd made such a point of warning Trace not to get serious?

His cell rang. Nikki's tone. He could have answered the call, but he was too damn angry. So angry, he'd pulled over on the side of the road not too far out of town. Listening to her voice mail telling him she wanted to explain made him ache with disappointment and embarrassment all over again, and he wanted to throw the damn cell out the window. She'd had the chance to explain when he was standing next to her in front of everyone.

Trace sat in the dark, trying to make sense of things. Was that guy still at the bar? She clearly hadn't wanted him there. Dammit. How was Trace supposed to run off in his righteous fury if Nikki needed him?

Maybe he was the biggest fool in Montana but he couldn't

just leave. She hadn't wanted Luis there, and no matter what, Trace wasn't about to drive off without knowing she was okay. For all he knew, Luis had abused her, and that's why she'd left him.

"Well, shit." Trace slammed his hand against the wheel. That was another possible angle. But she still should've told him. Trusted him with the truth.

He turned the ignition again, and made a U-turn to get himself back to the bar. To Nikki. It would be hell walking into the Watering Hole, but there was more at stake than his pride.

He needed to make sure she was safe.

"DON'T YOU GET IT? I'm not like that anymore. I worked all these years—"

"Luis, look, I'm happy for you," she said, as she stared down the street, hoping to spot Trace's truck. She didn't see it, but at least they weren't having this conversation in front of half the town. She turned back to Luis. "And I'm proud. You've done everything you said you would. But it's been a long time."

He snorted and curled his hands into fists. "You think it was easy getting out of that life?"

"I know it wasn't. It hasn't been easy for me, either. And I wasn't—"

"Using. Or in the gang."

She nodded. "Listen, what you did took courage. And you'll do great at the body shop. But not with me."

Luis exhaled sharply. "I suppose it was too much to hope for. But I had to try."

"It wouldn't work anymore. I'm not that girl."

He reached up and touched the side of her face before he turned and walked down the street. She watched him climb into his Chevy, then pulled out her cell phone and hit Trace's speed dial, still not sure what to say. Of course, it went to voice mail just as it had five minutes ago. She wouldn't leave another message. She'd already asked him to come back so she could explain.

Why hadn't she just said right then that Luis was lying? No, she should have told Trace the whole story. She'd been dreaming when she thought she could really have a new life, that all of her sins were in the past. She'd dared to think she didn't have to live and die in the same three square miles of her childhood. But she'd let her guilt, her shame, get the best of her.

She had to find him, to tell him the truth and to admit she'd been a fool for not telling him everything. She wasn't nearly as brave as he thought she was. The truth was, she'd been a coward, running from her past. Maybe she should keep on running. She'd take Wallace's money and start a whole new life, somewhere no one knew her. Now she knew better than to fall for a pair of green eyes and a broad chest. Love was for other people. Not for the likes of her.

Tears welled, and she swiped them away with the back of her hand. *Wallace, you win.*

Nikki's breath caught at the terrible thought. No. He wasn't right about her, dammit. She was better than that. Stronger. She'd made mistakes, and this one might just kill her, but this time she wouldn't be running from her mistake—the real mistake would be to run and leave the most amazing man she'd ever met.

The only thing she could do now was to own up to everything. To be the woman Trace thought she was. She'd stay, finish her night at work, knowing everyone in there would be staring and talking about her. But that didn't matter. She'd come too far to let the old Nikki have her way. The brave Nikki was going to walk back into that bar with her head up.

TRACE STOOD OUTSIDE the door to the Watering Hole, dreading the spectacle. Nothing a bunch of drunk cowboys liked more than a free show, and they'd already gotten the first act. He thought about waiting for the place to close, but screw that. His pride had cost him too much already. Now that he'd seen her truck was still there, he wasn't going to let anything stop him from walking inside and seeing for himself that Nikki wasn't in trouble.

As he pulled the door open, the music hit him like a wave, but just his luck, the goddamn song ended. Every eye was on him.

His gaze went to the bar, and there she was. She hadn't seen him yet, but the sudden silence made her turn. Her look of uncertainty and fear made the rest of the world disappear. He made it across the floor without feeling a step. "Are you okay?" he asked.

She nodded. "I was sixteen. I was hurting after Garret. I was an ass. I'm so sorry."

"So he was telling the truth?"

Her cringe made him ache. "No. Well, not exactly. We went over the border and got married. My mother had it annulled by the end of the week."

"Why didn't you just tell me? I thought you trusted me."

She let out a small whimper. "I do, but I was ashamed. I'd already told you some things about my past, but I was afraid to admit how crazy it had gotten. I'm not the girl next door."

The crack of a pool rack breaking apart split the quiet, and someone coughed, but Trace didn't care. "I know that," he said. "I don't want the girl next door. I want you, just the way you are."

"You don't, though. You don't know—"

"We sat in this very bar back in February, and you told me all I needed to hear about who you were. I was hooked. Still am. You're not the only one who's been holding back.

I should have told you before tonight." He leaned over and caught her hand. It was ice-cold and felt so fragile. "Rachel told me a long time ago that when I finally fell, I'd fall hard. I hate to admit it, but she was spot-on. I love you, Nikki. I kept telling myself I was too young to say those words, but not saying the words doesn't make it less true."

NIKKI OPENED HER MOUTH, but nothing came out. She was still too shocked. "Are you sure?"

"Well, hell, honey, just ask anyone here. You've got a lot of witnesses."

"Oh, God." Her hand covered her mouth as she realized where they were. They might as well have been standing in the middle of the street in broad daylight. No, this was worse. Jerry and Eli had turned their chairs away from their table to get a better view. Sadie at least pretended she wasn't listening. Nikki closed her eyes, wishing everyone but Trace would disappear.

"You gonna leave me hanging out here in the wind?"

Snapping her eyes open, she leaned forward, but she couldn't reach more than his hand over the bar. "What? No. Oh, no. Me, too. I mean, I'm pretty sure. That I love you."

He smiled. "I'll take it. I'm just glad you weren't halfway to Houston. I would have hated making that long drive to go get you. I shouldn't have stormed off."

"Oh, I knew you'd be back."

"How?"

"Something your mom said. Of all three boys, you're the most like your dad. You definitely have the McAllister pride, but you also have the McAllister honor." Nikki walked around the bar until she stood right in front of him. "I didn't know how it would turn out, but I knew you'd let me explain."

"My mom said that?" He looked stunned, a little emotional. "I'm like my dad?"

Nikki nodded. "She did."

"That's a hell of a thing to hear. Thank you. But I didn't come back because of honor, sweetheart." He pulled her close until she was pressed right up against him and he was looking straight into her eyes. "I came back because you're the best thing that's ever happened to me."

She pressed her lips together, trying hard not to cry. The only man who made a difference thought she was just fine the way she was. He loved her. He'd even said it in front of everybody.

When he kissed her, the whole place burst into applause, but she could still hear Sadie's gravelly voice saying, "It's about damn time."

* * * * *

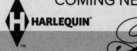

REQUEST YOUR FREE BOOKS!
2 FREE NOVELS PLUS 2 FREE GIFTS!

HARLEQUIN® Blaze®
red-hot reads!

YES! Please send me 2 FREE Harlequin® Blaze™ novels and my 2 FREE gifts (gifts are worth about $10). After receiving them, if I don't wish to receive any more books, I can return the shipping statement marked "cancel." If I don't cancel, I will receive 4 brand-new novels every month and be billed just $4.74 per book in the U.S. or $4.96 per book in Canada. That's a savings of at least 14% off the cover price. It's quite a bargain. Shipping and handling is just 50¢ per book in the U.S. and 75¢ per book in Canada.* I understand that accepting the 2 free books and gifts places me under no obligation to buy anything. I can always return a shipment and cancel at any time. Even if I never buy another book, the two free books and gifts are mine to keep forever.

150/350 HDN F4WC

Name	(PLEASE PRINT)	
Address		Apt. #
City	State/Prov.	Zip/Postal Code

Signature (if under 18, a parent or guardian must sign)

Mail to the Harlequin® Reader Service:
IN U.S.A.: P.O. Box 1867, Buffalo, NY 14240-1867
IN CANADA: P.O. Box 609, Fort Erie, Ontario L2A 5X3

Want to try two free books from another line?
Call 1-800-873-8635 or visit www.ReaderService.com.

* Terms and prices subject to change without notice. Prices do not include applicable taxes. Sales tax applicable in N.Y. Canadian residents will be charged applicable taxes. Offer not valid in Quebec. This offer is limited to one order per household. Not valid for current subscribers to Harlequin Blaze books. All orders subject to credit approval. Credit or debit balances in a customer's account(s) may be offset by any other outstanding balance owed by or to the customer. Please allow 4 to 6 weeks for delivery. Offer available while quantities last.

Your Privacy—The Harlequin® Reader Service is committed to protecting your privacy. Our Privacy Policy is available online at www.ReaderService.com or upon request from the Harlequin Reader Service.

We make a portion of our mailing list available to reputable third parties that offer products we believe may interest you. If you prefer that we not exchange your name with third parties, or if you wish to clarify or modify your communication preferences, please visit us at www.ReaderService.com/consumerschoice or write to us at Harlequin Reader Service Preference Service, P.O. Box 9062, Buffalo, NY 14269. Include your complete name and address.

Free Fall

"So you were, what, just a teenager when you left?" Jack asked.

Maggie tipped her chin up and looked directly at him. "I was almost nineteen. Old enough to be married."

He blanched. "Were you? Married?"

If he was going to be living around here, he would eventually learn the truth. Ten years wasn't nearly enough time for the locals to have forgotten. But there was no way she was going to fill him in on the sordid details. She'd endured enough humiliation at being jilted; the last thing she wanted was this man's pity.

"I came close," she finally said. "But we didn't go through with it."

"So you ran, and you didn't look back."

Maggie looked sharply at him, startled by his astuteness. "My leaving had nothing to do with that," she fibbed. "I simply decided to pursue my dream of becoming a photographer."

"So what about now? Is there someone waiting for you back in Chicago?"

She shook her head. "No. There's nobody like that in Chicago."

"Good."

And just like that, the air between them thrummed with

energy. Jack took a step toward her, and Maggie held her breath. There was something in his expression—something hot and full of promise—that made her heart thump heavily against her ribs, and heat slide beneath her skin. She couldn't remember the last time a man had made her feel so aware of herself as a woman. Reaching out, he traced a finger along her cheek.

"It's getting late. You should go to bed." His voice was low and Maggie thought it sounded strained.

Erotic images of the two of them, naked and entwined beneath her sheets, flashed through her mind.

In three weeks, she would return to Chicago, and the likelihood of ever seeing Jack Callahan again was zero. Did she have the guts to reach out and take what she wanted, knowing she couldn't keep it? She wasn't sure, and suddenly she didn't care.

Turning, she opened the back door to the house, and then looked at Jack. "Why don't you join me?"

Pick up FREE FALL by Karen Foley, available June 19 wherever you buy Harlequin® Blaze® books.

It's a bridal basket auction!

Forget baked goods and innocent picnics—
Margot Walker's "anonymous" basket is all about
risqué and reward! Eight pieces of paper are
tucked inside, each listing a different destination.
And each destination is an erotic promise....

Sexy cowboy Clint Barrows knows Margot is the
one who got away, and he's determined to find
out exactly what is in her basket...and to meet
each naughty adventure with one of his own!

Pick up

Lead Me On

by *Crystal Green*
available June 19 wherever you buy
Harlequin Blaze books.

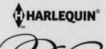